*Revising Romance*

# Revising Romance

*by*

MELANIE DUGAN

SUMACH
PRESS

NATIONAL LIBRARY OF CANADA CATALOGUING IN PUBLICATION

Dugan, Melanie
Revising romance / Melanie Dugan.

ISBN 1-894549-34-1

I. Title.

PS8557.U3214R48 2004     C813'.6     C2004-900661-4

Edited by Jennifer Glossop
Copy-edited by Lindsay Humphreys
Cover & Design by Elizabeth Martin
Cover image by Lori Richards

*Sumach Press acknowledges the support of the Canada Council for the Arts
and the Ontario Arts Council for our publishing program. We acknowledge
the financial support of the Government of Canada through the Book Publishing
Industry Development Program (BPIDP) for our publishing activities.*

ONTARIO ARTS COUNCIL
CONSEIL DES ARTS DE L'ONTARIO

Printed and bound in Canada

*Published by*

SUMACH PRESS

1415 Bathurst Street, Suite 202
Toronto ON Canada
M5R 3H8
*sumachpress@on.aibn.com*
*www.sumachpress.com*

*Dedication*

*To Don, Dugan and Hayden, and to my father, Hammond Dugan.*

*Acknowledgements*

I want to thank the following people for their help and support: my sisters Alison, Ann and Frances, and my brother John; Gisela Argyle; Julie Blunden, for her insights into the hidden lives of real-estate agents; Lori Richards, for the beautiful cover art that captures the book's spirit; Brian Henry, for his advice and support; Noelle Allen, for her part in bringing the book to fruition; Liz Martin, Lois Pike, Rhea Tregebov and Lindsay Humphreys and the team at Sumach Press. Finally, a huge thank you to Jennifer Glossop for all her contributions and for her editorial acumen.

# *Chapter 1*

THURSDAY

*Today's the day, today's the day* — I wake with this thought buzzing like a hyperactive bee in my brain. As consciousness dawns, I lie listening to the buzz, then it occurs to me: *the day for what?* I poke around in my memory banks, still sluggish with sleep, trying to recall what woke me with such urgency.

Then I remember. Today's Thursday, the day I meet Spencer Stone, best-selling author. I'll be shadowing Morris, the Senior Editor, as he polishes the manuscript of Spencer's long-awaited novel. In the three years I've worked at Hunter Press, I've edited a collection of essays and a couple of books on local history, but fiction is what really interests me. I'm hoping that after this, my boss will give me some novels to work on by myself.

Up and out of bed — out of futon, in fact. ("Still sleeping on the floor, I see," my mother observed sharply the first time she visited. "I thought people stopped doing that once they were adults.")

Knees, hips and various other joints voice their displeasure at being so rudely awakened as I stumble down the hallway and into the bathroom. I fumble for the light switch and am suddenly confronted by my reflection in the mirror. There are other ugly truths I'd prefer to deal with immediately on waking, but short of plastic surgery (an unlikely option; my dentist will attest to the fact that I never willingly submit to pain), what I see in the mirror is what I have to work with, forehead wrinkles and all.

So after my shower, I rub moisturizer into my forehead and attempt to modify the haystack hairstyle I'm sporting, trying instead for the casual windblown look, though I admit the distinction is a subtle one. After addressing my mortality this way — a little job I like to get out of the way first thing in the morning — I check the mirror again. Things are looking, if not better, at least slightly less rumpled. *Carpe diem,* I tell myself. *Or at least carpe coffee.* Onward and upward.

First stop: Emily's room. My ten year old daughter is the light of my life, but she is definitely not a morning person. I walk into her room and start peeling away the layers of sheets and blankets she sleeps under.

"Mo-om," she groans.

I'm not sure how she manages to get enough oxygen, curled up as she is like a gerbil beneath all that bedding, but she's alive every morning when I rouse her from hibernation.

After this first foray I go upstairs to make breakfast, which is to say push the button on the already-loaded automatic coffee maker.

The house I live in is a funky, three-tiered, loft-style number, a new interior jerry-built inside the shell of what was once an outbuilding of one of the larger homes on the block. Obviously, the updated interior was designed by someone who had no experience living with children. The bedrooms and bathroom are on the ground floor. Upstairs, where an open plan predominates, the living room blends into the kitchen. Those two rooms make up the second floor, and on the third floor is my study-cum-office.

Once the coffee maker is happily gurgling along, I check the clock: 7:27.

"Come on, Em," I call down the stairs. "Time to get moving."

No response.

"Em," I shout a bit louder. This prompts a muffled response, an undefined moan.

When she still hasn't appeared ten minutes later, I bellow, "Em, if you don't get moving, I'm going to have to come down there and pull you out of bed."

"Okay, okay," I hear her grumble.

I finish spreading peanut butter on bread, stashing an apple and a granola bar in her lunch bag, and still my daughter hasn't appeared. "Em!" I bellow.

"I'm coming," she says glumly, trudging up the stairs. I turn at the sound of her voice; her hair is a tangled mess, her eyes still heavy with sleep. My angel.

"I hate getting up this early," she grumbles. "Dad doesn't make me get up this early."

My heart twists painfully, but I try to keep my voice even. "Em, I'm not your dad, and you live with me. You know I have to get to work by 8:30 and your dad can start whenever he wants. Now eat your breakfast and then I'll comb your hair." I set a glass of milk and a peanut-butter-and-banana sandwich on the table, her breakfast of choice.

"If I lived with Dad, I could sleep until just before school starts."

"If you lived with Dad, you'd be eating yogurt for breakfast because he never remembers to do the shopping," I snap, and regret it instantly. Em hates it when we criticize each other. Her expression becomes guarded, withdrawn. "Sorry, sweetie," I say, rubbing her shoulder. "I'm just jumpy because I have a big meeting this morning. Your dad does a good job."

"That's okay, Mom," she says forgivingly. Now I feel like a real jerk. Then she grins. "You're right. I hate yogurt." The cloud has passed; we're friends again.

Half an hour later I drop Emily off at her before-school program and carry on to the office. Hunter Press is known in the trade as Predator Press because of its aggressive policy of chasing down any book that looks like a potential money-maker, which makes for a rather peculiar backlist. We've got a half-dozen kids' books of the sort grandparents buy because they look as though they'll be good for the grandchildren. These books feature uplifting morals, no hint of violence or sex and positively no humour. I know, because Emily has one or two such books. These books never get picked up by the kids who receive them from Grammy or Grampa. Instead they languish in the distant, shadowy reaches of a bookcase, collecting dust.

Hunter also has a couple of dozen titles on New Age health practices and philosophical systems and an academically oriented series of essays on the early history of microwave technology. Each of these lines represents projects that my boss, Hilliard Robinson, was sure would make the money roll in; each was adopted with great enthusiasm; each has quietly slipped into the obscurity of the backlist.

Our seasonal selection can be an equally odd mix. Over time, Hill has stumbled on a combination of topics that seem to sell consistently. As a result, each season we produce one book in the Modern Music Line about a rock-and-roll singer, a book of local history, a cookbook and perhaps a mildly sensationalistic biography. These lines have proven to be consistently profitable. The Modern Music Line sells especially well in the United States, generating a steady trickle of American dollars into Hunter's coffers.

With a nod toward capital *L* Literature, we also publish a line of literary fiction and a series of poetry books which the critics love and the buying public largely ignores. My guess is, Hill feels these literary efforts give our list cachet and maybe get us a few brownie points in the critics' estimation. And, of course, he's hoping to find the next hot young writer whose work will rocket into the stratosphere, receiving critical and popular approbation and generating a healthy surplus in the company's bank account.

Lots of people, my mother included, think publishing sounds glamorous. I'm not sure why they imagine that hanging out with impecunious writers, some embittered by long years of rejection and subsistence living, constitutes glamour, but I do my best to sustain the illusion. Sometimes I think my job, with its nimbus of what looks like excitement and drama but is really sheer panic at yet another fast-approaching deadline, is the one reason my mother still talks to me. When I first got this job, Jim, then my husband, now my ex, laughed.

"What?" I said.

"You, an editor?"

"Why not?"

"You'll admit grammar isn't your strong point. You do have a tendency to always split infinitives and jumble sentences up."

"So I talk fast and mix things up," I said. "It's just that my tongue has trouble keeping up with my brain. I edit slowly and know a run-on sentence when I come across one."

Jim snorted.

It's a lovely morning in late September; the sky is clear, the air brisk. At 8:20, I breeze into the office. Jerri, the receptionist (official title: Office Manager — Hill likes to give us important-sounding titles because he thinks it makes us take our work more seriously), gives me a wave, phone already glued to her ear. Thank goodness, no chitchat to endure. I wave back, mouthing a silent "Hi," and scoot over to my desk, out of her range, as quickly as I can.

I like Jerri. She's a huge improvement over our last receptionist, whose demeanour reminded me of a bad-tempered Pekinese — yap, snap, yap, snap. In contrast, Jerri is very sweet. She reminds me of Em — an older Em — and sometimes I just want to ruffle her hair the way I do Em's. Jerri is in her mid-twenties. She's only been with Hunter a few months. We get along well, but there's something vague and out-of-focus about her. She makes me think of those old movies where they would smear petroleum jelly on the camera lens to give the heroine a soft, gauzy aura. Jerri looks this way most of the time; worse, I suspect the inside of her head is out-of-focus, too.

Hill hired her fresh from university. She came equipped with four earrings in each ear, a ring in her right eyebrow and a cute little diamond stud in her nose. She has hinted at piercings in other parts of her anatomy. I don't know — I don't ask. I am fundamentally a physical coward and don't want to know about anything that might be painful.

Jerri has a fluctuating sexual identity, and I'll admit to having more curiosity about this since, unlike the piercings, her explorations in this area don't seem to involve pain.

"I'm not sure if I'm straight or bi," she confessed to me once during a coffee break. I realized afterward that it was relief I was feeling, relief that I'd never actually had to resolve that question — my preference has always been entirely clear to me.

She's talked to me occasionally about her various *tendres*. At one point she was seeing a woman who worked for the phone company, but Jerri called it quits after a few months. "She had all these hang-ups," Jerri told me.

After Hill interviewed Jerri for the job, he told me how useful her English degree would be. If she were working in Editorial he might be right — and she does seem to have an awful lot of questions about what my job entails — but her degree has in no way equipped her to do the job of office manager. We routinely run out of paper, pens, envelopes and other essentials. She made coffee once; subsequently Janine, the bookkeeper, and I took her aside and impressed on her just how happy we'd be to take responsibility for that chore (I was awake until two a.m. that night). She has yet to master the finer points of office protocol. When I asked her to courier a package of photos to the printers yesterday, I essentially had to walk her through the process step by step, filling out the waybill, looking up the courier's phone number and reminding her to call the printers to tell them the package was on its way. She often neglects, for instance, to note the caller's name when taking telephone messages, as if I'm supposed to intuit their identity telepathically. And this morning I find in the middle of my desk just such a phone message.

I drift over to Jerri's desk in what I hope is a calm, self-possessed manner. Evincing just the slightest flicker of curiosity — I don't want to make it seem too important, or she might panic and forget entirely — I ask, "Do you happen to recall who left this message?"

Jerri looks up at me slightly sheepishly. Despite my attempts to conceal it, she senses my irritation. "Oh." She smiles uneasily. "It was a lady with a furry sort of voice."

"Furry voice?" I raise my eyebrows, consider for a moment. "No," shaking my head, "can't place the furry voice."

Her hands flap ineffectually in front of her. "Her name, you know, is sort of like 'rock.'" Doubt pitches her voice higher, makes her sound more tentative.

"Rock?" I repeat thoughtfully. "Roche, perhaps?" I suggest. She shakes her head. "Rick? Rack?" More head-shaking.

"No, no, not Rack." A frown of concentration puckers her forehead, the ring in her eyebrow shifts. "I can't remember. But what I wanted to know was whether it wasn't time to be sending out the review copies of *Tectonic Shift?*" she says, mentioning this season's poetry book.

"That's my job, Jerri, and I'm on top of it. I couriered the review copies last Thursday. You were out of the office — wasn't that the day you had your doctor's appointment? — and I wanted to get them out quickly. But what I really need to know right now is who called this morning."

"Hmm." She takes the message from my hand and stares at it, as if under her prolonged scrutiny the slip of paper will reveal its secret.

Devil-may-care, I toss off, "Stone?"

"No, not Stone," she mutters.

When I haven't stumbled onto the answer after five minutes, I give up and retire to my desk to puzzle over the caller's identity. A few minutes later, I hear a shriek of triumph.

"Crystal," Jerri calls. "That's it, Crystal. That's who called."

Does she do this just to make me crazy? It seems extraneous at this point to ask who Crystal might be, since I know no Crystal, don't remember speaking to a Crystal and can't imagine why a Crystal would call me. By now I've had enough. The whole exchange is making me slightly dizzy and I really just want to get back to work.

Today I want to avoid dizzy. I'd like to avoid Jerri, too, until after the meeting with Spencer Stone. I want to be sharp for the meeting, I want to be astute, incisive — but what's this sitting on the corner of my desk?

I feel my stomach start to knot. What seems to be a small pile — one couldn't call it a package — of crumpled polka-dot wrapping paper sits on my desk, topped by a plaid ribbon. I feel vertiginous just looking at it. Propped against this assemblage is an envelope with "Elaine" written on the front in Jerri's handwriting.

Too late it occurs to me — my birthday? Surely not; isn't it next week? I glance at my page-a-day desk calendar. I simply haven't changed the damn thing for a week. Jerri has, as usual, managed to get it not-quite-right — tomorrow's the big day. I balance on the cusp of being thirty-five years old.

I've been having trouble with years lately. It took me a while to get on track after my last birthday — for months afterward I was telling everyone I was thirty-three. Completely inadvertently, I might add. It wasn't until Em overheard me one day and said, "That can't be right, Mom. I'm ten and you were twenty-four when you had me, right?" Thank you for that reality check, Em. So here I am, another year older — thirty-*five,* to be exact.

I sense Jerri hovering by my left elbow, bubbling in anticipation. I turn and grin at her. "You really shouldn't have," I say. She has no idea how heartfelt those words are.

"Open it," she says, with barely suppressed excitement, gesturing toward the package on my desk. I do as I'm told.

"How nice." The card is of the flowery genre, the sentiments inside are as well, expressed in aggressively rhymed couplets with five fiercely marching feet per line.

Next I unwrap the package; within rests a coffee mug. One with words on it, no less. *Today is the first day of the rest of your life.* Why does that sound like a threat?

"What a thoughtful gift," I say. "I've never had one like it before."

"I think it's important to always be trying new things," she says. Do I hear a subtext, or is that my imagination talking? She's the one with the English degree, not me.

"Thank you, Jerri." I turn and give her a quick hug. "I was thinking my old one was getting a bit shabby. I'll christen this one right now." I walk over to the coffee maker, pour myself some coffee, and add some milk to it for calcium's sake — one must keep osteoporosis at bay.

Satisfied, Jerri disappears, wreathed in smiles, to answer the ringing telephone. Back at my desk I consider the mug. A thoughtful gift, but proof positive Jerri's from another planet. On *my* planet the cup would say: *Another day older and deeper in debt.*

This kind of thinking used to drive Jim crazy. "Jeez, Elaine," he'd say. "The mug is just a gift. You take everything too personally."

He may have had a point. I'd like to be more objective, to be able to approach life in the third person: *Elaine Salter, petite, vivacious, really pulled-together-looking, embarks on another day at work, organizer in hand, coffee mug at the ready.* (I like "embarks," it sounds so organized, as if a military campaign is in progress.) But let's be realistic: objective I'm not, or pulled-together. As my mother is all too willing to point out. "Elaine, dear, if you'd only co-ordinate your accessories, you'd achieve a much more polished, professional appearance." This *is* how my mother talks. *How* she manages to do it with a straight face, I have no idea. She must have learned it at those business seminars she's always attending.

It's not until I sense Hill standing beside me that I realize I've drifted into a daydream of a sartorially splendid me: beautifully turned-out, perfectly accessorized, ready to take on the world — or deal with a recalcitrant author, whichever comes first.

"Production meeting at 9:15," Hill says. Then he turns on his heel and disappears into his office. Oh, right, there's the reminder, scribbled in my calendar.

Which gives me half an hour to pull things together and determine where my various projects stand. Then Hill, Morris and I — the Editorial department — will adjourn to the conference room and figure out what's on schedule and what we need to panic about.

Morris arrives just before 9:00, setting his briefcase down on his desk. He and I share a large room separated from Jerri's reception area by an archway. Hill's office opens off ours, the only one in the place with a door, which Hill shuts frequently — the better to toil in splendid isolation, uninterrupted by the ringing of phones, the babble of small talk and the occasional author who wanders in with a new project in mind or with questions about his last royalty statement.

"How's it going?" I ask.

"Fine, fine."

"Production meeting in fifteen minutes," I tell him.

"And don't forget we're meeting Spencer at 10:00," he adds.

"I'm looking forward to that. It should be interesting."

Morris nods in a preoccupied way, gathering his neatly arranged files from his immaculately tidy desk. I glance at his desk enviously and follow him down the hall.

Morris is a sweetie: tall, dark, willowy and good-natured. He's also just a tad obsessive-compulsive, which serves him well in his capacity as Senior Editor, and a bit high-strung, which doesn't. A wizard with words, he can undangle a participle or reunite a split infinitive more gracefully than anyone I've worked with.

When I first started working at Hunter as Office Manager, before Hill bumped me into Editorial, the press was producing around a dozen titles a year. Morris edited the majority of these, line by line, impeccably. Over time, Hill has pushed the total higher and brought me in to help with the load. I've watched Morris do his heroic best to keep up. His shoulders are more bowed than they once were, and there's a tic in his left cheek that wasn't there when I first started, but he always manages to get the work done and the books out on deadline.

The conference room where we're meeting is at the front of the building. When the building was new and Kingston a flourishing metropolis, the conference room was the front parlour. Both building and city have settled into querulous old age, the one complaining when toilets are flushed and too many lights turned on, the other protesting about a failing infrastructure.

High-ceilinged, with a fluted plaster medallion where an elaborate light once hung, the room is spacious and airy. French doors at one end open onto what was once a courtyard and is now merely a patch of weedy grass bordered by a front walk, pitted from years of heaving winter frosts.

Morris and I enter and find Hill seated on the far side of the large oak table that dominates the room.

Hill has earned his nickname: physically and temperamentally, he resembles a hill. Short and squat, he's considerably wider at the middle than at the top, and when I search for words to describe him, "intractable," "intransigent" and "immovable" spring quickly to mind. "Ursine," too, given his predilection for spending time sequestered in his office like a bear hibernating, out of reach of authors and their demands, complaints and questions. Periodically he emerges to growl at one of us in the outer office, demand a file or grumble about what he feels is an unreasonable request on the part of one of our authors. Then he withdraws again.

He's not much older than I am — somewhere in his early forties — but the gap between us seems wider than a mere eight or nine years. Maybe it's his thinning black hair and thickening waist; maybe it's the stodgy clothes he favours, all baggy and brown. I know he has an adolescent son and daughter from a defunct marriage only because once in a while he mentions having seen them on the weekend. They never darken the door of the press. His ex-wife is similarly invisible, although she phones him now and then to discuss the kids.

From bits of information he's dropped, I know it was not his ambition to be a publisher. I think he sometimes wonders how he ended up one. Indications are, he started out in journalism, did some teaching and somehow ended up taking over Hunter Press as it teetered on the edge of bankruptcy. He figured he'd drag it out of the red into the black and then unload it for a small profit. He turned it around financially, but before he could divest himself of the company, it started to slip into the red again and he had to scramble to haul it back. This has been the cycle for the fifteen years he's owned the company.

When he sees us in the doorway, Hill taps the pile of paper in front of him into order. "Have a seat," he says.

This isn't Hill in a good mood, charming, playful and cracking jokes. This is grim Hill. It looks as though it will be a long meeting. I settle in for the duration, Morris beside me.

"I have some good news," Hill begins, not sounding as if this is the case. "Yesterday I finally took delivery of Kaz Sachs's manuscript." Sachs is a rock-and-roller whose life and music are both, by all reports, focussed on sex and drugs. His autobiography is a natural for the Modern Music Line and has been promised in our catalogue for a year now.

"Unfortunately," Hill continues, "this guy has fried his synapses so badly he can't remember last week, let alone his childhood. This" — he pats the stack of paper in front of him — "is going to require a lot of work. Morris, I'm going to pass the *River Lore Anthology* on to you, along with the Inuit short-story collection. Elaine, you'll pick up the poetry book."

Silence falls on the room. I glance sideways at Morris, who has turned an interesting shade of pale green. I'm thinking: *a poetry book isn't too bad, I can probably manage that.* Then I hear Morris's chair screech on the floor.

"Two more titles?" he says, sounding strangled. He's jumped to his feet and is leaning forward slightly, as if he's about to pounce on Hill. "You're dumping two more titles on me? Are you out of your mind?"

Hill says nothing.

"When I first started working here, I handled ten books a year. You pushed it to twelve, then to sixteen. Now it's almost twenty," Morris says, his voice dangerously quiet. "You pile on the work, and I manage to get through it. But I can't take on more two titles this late in the season and do anything approaching a reasonable job, Hill. There are limits."

Hill remains silent.

"It can't be done," Morris says, his voice rising sharply. "It's not humanly possible."

Still Hill sits wordless, staring at Morris.

After several moments, Morris throws up his hands. "Fine. That's it. I'm out of here." And he is; he turns and walks out the door, leaving Hill and me looking at each other across the table.

For maybe three seconds we sit like that, then my eyes waver and fall to the papers in front of me. When I glance up, Hill is staring at the door through which Morris exited, his expression opaque.

Then, as if nothing has just detonated in front of us, Hill turns to me and says in an even tone — this calmness in the aftermath of Morris's explosion makes my blood run cold — "Well, Elaine. I guess that leaves you."

# Chapter 2

"ME?" I HOPE I'M THE ONLY ONE who hears the squeak of panic in my voice. My question's rhetorical; there is no one in the room but Hill and me. I sit in stunned confusion; isn't Hill going to go after Morris and try to persuade him to stay?

Hill doesn't respond to my single syllable response. He busies himself tidying his already tidy pile of paper. "You've been with the press — what? — three years?" he asks without looking at me.

I nod, not trusting my voice.

"And in Editorial about a year now?"

"Yes."

"I didn't plan on bringing you up to speed so soon," he mutters, as much to himself as me, it seems. "But considering the situation ..." his voice trails off.

I'm not sure what it would be politic to say, so I say nothing and sit, trying to look intelligent.

"There is Jerri," he continues, as if weighing the possibilities. "But she hasn't been here long and doesn't really know the ropes." Again he lapses into quiet thoughtfulness.

As if he's reached a decision, Hill straightens. "Okay," he says in a firmer voice. "I think we can safely assume Morris won't be back. I'll restructure the company. You're now Senior Editor."

Hill's comment catches me off-guard. *This is a good thing,* I tell myself, feeling dazed. *The problem is, it's happening in a bad way.* I didn't realize the company had any structure at all, aside from Hill sitting at the apex while the rest of us beetle around below like industrious insects. I'm tempted to ask whether I'm going to get a raise in salary commensurate with my expanded responsibilities.

One look at Hill's expression convinces me to stifle the impulse.

"There are a few points I want to clarify," Hill continues. "The first is, Hunter is experiencing cash flow problems."

"Cash flow problems?" I echo, trying to keep the alarm I feel out of my voice.

"The press is very sound financially, and there will be some grant money coming in presently," he rushes to reassure me. "We're just short of cash right now. I'm counting on Spencer Stone's novel to remedy that problem — Spencer and Kaz Sachs together. We've got to get both of them into the stores well before Christmas. Do you understand?"

I nod.

"You're looking at a tight production schedule," he says.

*You?* I think. What about *we?*

"That's two months to edit, copy-edit, proof and print the book — but it has to be done. We have advance orders in the neighbourhood of five thousand copies for Spencer's novel, which makes it a huge best-seller by our standards. Hunter Press needs this novel to fly."

"Right." I nod.

"So Spencer's novel is your priority. I'm assuming that Morris has been on top of things and there's not much left to do."

I nod again, although Hill doesn't seem to be paying attention to me. He's staring into the middle distance, a speculative expression on his face. "I'll be trying to fix this mess." He waves his hand at the stack of paper. "If you need help, use Jerri. Okay?"

"Okay," I say without conviction. I suspect an individual pulled at random off the street might be more useful than our receptionist. The time I'll have to spend explaining and double-checking any work she may do will be time out of my already busy schedule. And I'm not exactly eager to be her mentor, either, if it's going to put my job in jeopardy in the long run.

"And you have a week."

It takes a moment for me to process this. "A week?" Again my voice sounds like it needs oiling.

"A week." He nods.

He's got to be kidding. I mean, I did salvage that travel guide last month, slashing and restructuring the essays until they made sense and wouldn't get people hopelessly lost, all of this over the howls of the seven writers involved. But Spencer's novel? I mean, I'm sure Morris has done his usual superlative job and a thorough substantive edit has already been completed. I imagine Spencer and Morris bent over the table in the conference room or in Spencer's minimalist home office, Morris offering carefully phrased suggestions, Spencer giving a considering nod. A quick pencil stroke here, a swift scribble there. If Spencer has in fact taken Morris's comments into account and revised accordingly, then all the characters will be in place, clearly drawn and acting together well as an ensemble. They don't have to be adorable; they must be engaging. The narrative has been shaped so it flows smoothly, and any egregious anomalies or enormous implausibilities have been dealt with. By this point the big stuff should have been sorted out by Morris and Spencer and the manuscript I will be working with should be a nice, tight piece of writing that is almost ready to go.

But *almost* ready isn't ready; there are still the finishing-up chores: grammar and spelling checks; I have to ensure there are no sudden changes of gender, ethnicity or locale, and no characters left twisting in the wind without a role to play — which sometimes happens in transition from one draft to the next. Not a major edit, but not a job to rush through in a week, especially if what we're aiming for is excellence.

Hill can't be serious. I look over: he is serious.

"But —"

"No buts, Elaine. At least Spencer can write. With Kaz —" He shakes his head. "It's like giving a monkey a word processor and hoping it will come up with something. Spencer's novel is in the catalogue. We've got orders. It has to be in the bookstores before Christmas or we miss the biggest retail period of the year, and we can't afford that."

"No." *Maybe he's right,* I tell myself. *If the manuscript's already in good shape, a week might be just enough time for a thorough copy-edit.*

"Now, the reason Spencer stays with us, Elaine," Hill says, leaning forward for emphasis, "is because of the personal attention he gets here that he wouldn't get at a bigger publishing house. You take his calls, you answer his questions, you calm his worries. When he wants something, he gets it. Do you understand? We can't afford to have him jump ship."

"What Spencer wants, Spencer gets," I say.

"Your job is to keep him happy and make sure we have a bestseller."

*Oh, no problem,* I think. *That'll be a breeze. And while I'm at it, want to see me walk on water?*

"Get Morris's copy of the manuscript. It's probably on his desk. I know you've got a meeting set up with Spencer later today. Don't tell him Morris has left. Authors get nervous when their editor disappears suddenly. I don't care what you have to say, just keep Spencer focussed on the book. You and I will meet in a week. At that time I want the book fully edited, keyed, with the text ready to be dumped — and not into the garbage, into pages. All right?" There's a steely glint in his blue eyes.

"All right."

*Great. Just great.* Back at my desk I contemplate my coffee cup. The threat inscribed on it has come true: here is the rest of my life, and it's not looking too good. I should have stayed in bed when I had the chance. Let this be a lesson.

The first thing I have to do is locate the damn manuscript — just a small labour, not one of the big ones, like giving birth. Why isn't this thought a relief?

Jerri is in a flutter. She scurries over to my desk. "What happened?" she whispers loudly. "Morris just came stomping into the office, then five minutes later he went stomping out."

"He quit."

"Morris quit?"

*Am I working in an echo chamber?* "Yup," I reply.

"Why?"

"Long story." I hear Hill's footsteps in the hall. It's probably not wise to give her the full story right now. "Tell you later."

Morris's desk shows signs of his sudden departure: drawers yawn open, papers spill across it in disorganized heaps. He's left behind his coffee cup *(Editors do it punctually)* but taken the postcard of the Nova Scotia shoreline from his most recent vacation. He's also left his page-a-day calendar with "mtg.: S. Stone, 10" scribbled on today's date. I check my watch — I have fifteen minutes before Spencer arrives.

I dig through the piles of paper looking for Morris's copy of the manuscript. I don't want the poetry, pass also on the academic treatise by Dr. So-and-So. Surely Morris hasn't taken the manuscript with him in a fit of vengeance?

I tear the desk apart to no avail. There's no sign of Spencer's novel, not a word, not a punctuation mark. My attention lights on the drawers. I slide into Morris's chair and my fingers fly through the hanging file folders labelled in Morris's tiny perfect handwriting. Author questionnaires; form letters; authors' files and photos in alphabetical order; press kits for various books Morris worked on, arranged chronologically with the most recent first — but the novel is a no-show.

Spencer will be here any minute. *What am I going to do?* I flop back in the chair, and that's when I see it, on the bookshelf to the left of Morris's desk, wedged between a dictionary and a thesaurus — a lone file folder. My heart drumming a nervous tattoo, I pluck the file from its resting place. Just as I read *Stone, Spencer,* Jerri announces from the reception area, "Professor Stone is here to see you, Elaine."

I jump up and cast one last quick glance around. I stand, sans manuscript, clutching to my chest Morris's file folder, worryingly slender for all the notes and correspondence between Morris and Spencer that I hope it holds — but at this moment, my only hope — and turn as Hunter Press's best-selling author follows Jerri into the room.

"Mr. Stone," I say, extending my right hand with what I hope seems like pleased confidence. "Elaine Salter. How do you do?"

His shiny, tousled hair is the colour of hay; his eyes are dark. I'd guess he's about my age, maybe a few years older. He wears a black leather jacket, a charcoal grey shirt and a narrow black tie. His glasses are of the academic horn-rimmed kind. I realize he'd fit some women's picture of the intense artistic type, but not mine. If I weren't on the verge of hyperventilating from panic, I'd be tempted to slap him on the arm and say, "Hi, Spence, how you doing?" just to take the mickey out of him. I resist.

"If you'll just give me a moment." I scramble over to my own desk and grab a pen and a pad of paper. "We'll be meeting in the conference room." I flash him a smile. Spencer doesn't respond.

As I walk down the hall, I am a battleground for trepidation and curiosity — as well as the previously mentioned panic. It's getting a bit crowded inside me.

Not only does Spencer sell well, he is the press's most highly acclaimed author. "Highly acclaimed" — I hate that phrase. Whenever I encounter it in the vicinity of an author's name or the title of a book, my hackles rise. Exactly *how* highly acclaimed, I want to know. How are we to measure the height of this acclaim — in yards or metres? But it's true his work does generate a lot of praise. Every few years he publishes a collection of short stories to a torrent of favourable reviews. His pieces are artful and exquisitely constructed; the language is masterful, the images superbly wrought.

"Translucent prose," is what one critic said about his last book. The part of my brain involved in promotion and publicity notes that it would be a good quote to run on the book jacket. I'm not certain what translucent writing is, but the phrase has a nice ring to it and I'll grant there is an austere tone to his prose, an exactitude of phrase and syntax, the precision of which makes me feel claustrophobic.

I admire his writing but must admit, after I've spent time in one of his short stories, I'm overwhelmed by the urge to run out and buy a paperback with a cover illustration of a woman dressed in a flimsy garment rushing headlong from a sinister darkened building, replete with turrets, towers and bad atmosphere.

People of a certain level of income and education feel that to be taken seriously, they must have a copy of Spencer's most recent book lying around the house in full view of all visitors. Whether they read the book after they buy it is a moot point.

Yes — for Spencer, critics trot out all the usual superlatives and then invent some. But here's the rub: Spencer's reputation is built on a book he's never published, a book I have to be able to hand to Hill in a week.

For years Spencer's been "working on a novel." Rumours swirl around this project like flies around a cow pie. Every once in a while Spencer releases a section or two of the work-in-progress to a friend — when this happens, the whispers reach a crescendo. "Brilliant," say the people who have been thus privileged; "revolutionary," they say in tones of hushed awe, as if the experience has been a religious one.

It was on the basis of these rumours that Hill first agreed to take a look at the fifteen short stories Spencer submitted twelve years ago. Only two of the stories had seen publication at that time, and Spencer had no track record to speak of, so it was a gamble when Hill decided to collect twelve of the stories and publish them as a book. The acclaim for *Voices Raised* was resounding, and led to the publication, two years later, of Spencer's second collection of short stories. So it went.

Now, more than a decade after *Voices Raised* was received so enthusiastically and in the wake of equally positive responses to *Song in Shadow, Lost Harmonic* and his other collections, we have run the elusive novel to ground.

I met Spencer once before (it will be interesting to see if he remembers) when I visited his house with Morris. I had recently started working at Hunter, and Hill thought it would be good for me to meet the authors. Morris had an Editorial meeting arranged, so Hill told him to take me along. It was shortly after our move to town. Because of all the changes, Em, never a good sleeper, had started waking up frequently at night once again. The visit was a quick one and most of it passed in a blur.

I remember the inside of Spencer's house as a series of glaring white and off-white rooms. The place was spare and uncluttered; order reigned in his house as it does in his writing. In this subdued atmosphere, every time I opened my mouth I felt like I was shouting. In fact, the place made me *want* to shout "NICE PLACE YOU GOT HERE," since it was clear such quiet elegance cried out to be noticed. But I didn't make a scene. I've learned in the course of thirty-five years how to override these impulses ... most of the time. Not all of the time, which may have contributed to the demise of my marriage.

So I behaved myself and perched on the edge of a firm stream-lined modern sofa, all pillows and narrow pale grey stripes, while Spencer and Morris discussed a few details of fact. Light poured into the room through uncurtained windows set high in the walls, bounced off the bone-white paint job and gave me a headache. Or maybe I'd missed my mid-morning coffee. By the time the two of them had resolved some salient points (what colour *were* refrigerators in the 1950s?), my head was swimming. When I stood to leave, the room swooned around me.

Since I hadn't been in town long, I was unaware of the rumours that perennially swirl around Spencer. He registered, through a haze of headache and sleep deprivation, as pale and distant. There was a sang-froid to him, what might have been interpreted as an hauteur, an air of mystery — not the type to set my heart fluttering, but who can answer for the tastes of others?

Over the last few years, as I've made friends and built networks of acquaintance here, I've heard lots about him. Some women walk in beauty — Spencer walks cloaked in a cloud of gossip. I've heard tales of graduate students, faculty wives and research assistants left broken in his wake. There have been descriptions of tear-stained faces, midnight phone calls to friends, all manner of dramas. How much of this is true, I've never attempted to determine — I have other demands on my time. But his reputation does add a frisson of intrigue, a soupçon of excitement to the prospect of working with him.

When that excitement flares into apprehension, as it does now, I comfort myself with the knowledge that he's a known quantity and I'm a grown-up. I can handle the situation.

At the door to the conference room, I stand aside and let Spencer go in before me. He brushes past, sits down and sets his briefcase on the table. He pulls out a tattered file folder containing a pile of paper about an inch and a half thick and sets it on the table. Two elastic bands wrapped vertically and horizontally around the file keep the sheets of paper from spilling out of the folder. Little yellow Post-it Notes emerge like truncated fingers from the pages. This is a *bad* sign, since it suggests he's been fiddling with the manuscript, an activity to be firmly discouraged at this point in the process. We do not need any last-minute changes, no abrupt narrative detours or unexpected revelations.

I'm tempted to scoop up the file folder, slap away his hands — I imagine them grabbing at the manuscript in a proprietorial way — and bolt from the room. *Don't you understand?* I want to tell him. *Your job is over; the story's told. Now it's my turn to tidy up details, tie up loose ends. Just let me get on with it.*

Spencer glances around, a frown knotting his forehead. "Where's Morris?" he asks. I sense a note of irritation. He has a low-pitched voice and sounds hoarse, as if he's got a sinus infection or the beginnings of a cold; or maybe this is the male version of husky sultriness.

"Morris is ... on vacation," I say, hoping he won't notice the instant's hesitation it takes me to improvise for the absent Morris, hoping he won't immediately storm out to quiz Hill about this. I mime irritation — Morris, that scoundrel, taking a break at a time like this!

Spencer's eyes flicker over to me. They narrow. He gives me an appraising look.

"Vacation?" he says after a moment's pause — the same delay you get on long-distance phone calls, as if it's taken a while for my words to penetrate other, more important concerns. "He didn't mention anything about going on vacation at our last meeting."

Change tack. "It's a sabbatical, really." I pitch my voice low and confiding. "He's been under a lot of pressure recently, and Hill thought ..." I let the sentence drift off, shrugging vaguely, suggesting without saying outright how fragile poor Morris is. "I've taken over some of his responsibilities, but if you'd prefer to work with Hill" — I rush ahead — "I'm sure he'd be happy to make any changes you want."

Will Hill be happy if he has to do the edit himself? *In a pig's eye,* as Em is fond of saying, as in *I doubt it;* as in her response to my "Young women shouldn't wear too much makeup, Em, it makes them look cheap." *In a pig's eye, Mom. Look at Beyoncé. Cheap? I don't think so.* I haven't traced the etymology of the phrase.

Even when he's on his best behaviour, which he absolutely would be with Spencer, Hill has a gruffness to his manner that can bruise tender egos. He's also moody — charming sometimes, taciturn others, and sometimes the transition takes place in minutes, not hours. I've seen him transform a couple of our more delicate authors into nervous wrecks.

Instead of responding to my suggestion, Spencer turns his attention back to his manuscript. "No, that's all right," he says. "I'm sure you're competent. Otherwise Hill wouldn't have assigned you to me."

*Competent?* Well, thank you for that rousing vote of confidence, Mr. Stone. I'll try not to let your praise go to my head.

I set my coffee cup, pad of paper and file folder on the table and take a seat kitty-corner to Spencer.

When I moved to this town five years ago and found that having a thorough and complete knowledge of the Dewey Decimal system as well as two years' experience at one of the country's largest magazines in no way qualified me to find employment here, I did a stint at secretarial school. Along with courses in keyboarding, filing and Dictaphone, students were required to take a class called Psychology in the Workplace, where nuggets of wisdom along the lines of "Sitting directly opposite a person establishes a confrontational relationship; to create an atmosphere of co-operation, sit *beside* the person," were handed out. I'm always one for upping the co-operation quotient, so I apply this gem whenever possible. I'm not completely convinced of its efficacy though. It seems to me that an uncooperative prima donna is an uncooperative prima donna whether you sit across from him or on top of him, but I figure it's worth a try.

With Spencer bent over his manuscript, I take the opportunity to open the file folder labelled *Stone, S.,* and I am only partially successful in stifling an exclamation. Spencer glances up, frowning. I manage to shift my initial gasp of surprise into a cough.

"Sorry," I pat my chest. "Allergies." He turns back to his reading.

*Morris, you rat!* The file is empty, save for a single sheet covered in his cramped, scribbled notes; notes detailing Spencer's evasions and equivocations — in short, what amounts to Spencer's refusal to hand over the manuscript. *That's all right,* I tell myself. Morris wouldn't have had to have the manuscript in hand. Probably they've passed earlier drafts back and forth, and the version sitting in front of Spencer is the final draft that just requires a careful copy-edit.

My eyes bead on the stack of paper sitting placidly beside Spencer. No great distance away, but just out of easy reach. I turn back to Morris's notes. The entries end abruptly a few days ago.

I glance up; Spencer's still reading, pointedly disregarding me. I lock a smile on my face and clear my throat. "Well," I say brightly, "according to this, once I have your manuscript in hand, everything will be on track." I ease around the corner, slightly closer to Spencer's file folder.

At this comment Spencer turns to me, a gloomy expression on his face. "Sorry if I was a bit terse," he says, and shakes his head. "I'm having trouble with the beginning of the novel. I just don't think it starts strongly enough. So I've gone back and reworked the first third of it. I wish Morris were here. He's such a close reader ..." Spencer sighs deeply. "I'm really not sure this is ready to go."

"Not ready to go?" Echo chamber — now I sound like Jerri. "Of course it's ready to go. *Almost* ready to go," I amend. "Morris" — I indicate the folder — "seems to have every confidence in the project." *Liar, liar, pants on fire,* a voice sings in my head.

"I don't know." Spencer shakes his head ruefully. "I'm not sure." Another deep sigh. "Maybe if I had six more months."

*"Six more months?"* My voice is doing that high squeaky thing again. Is that my professional life flashing before my eyes? Smile and nod encouragingly. Don't give any indication that what you want right now is a stiff gin and tonic, hold the tonic. Murmur words of sympathy and encouragement as you plot how best to separate manuscript from author without appearing to.

Magicians, it occurs to me, have it easy. They merely have to make objects disappear, whisk them off into oblivion — *now you see it, now you don't.* I, however, must effect removal while the object is still in sight. I take a deep breath and nod, scooting still closer to the pile of paper and snaking my arm around it. In one quick motion, I guide it over in front of me.

"You know," I say feelingly, "in my experience, writers are usually their own worst critics. They're too aware of what they feel are their shortcomings, and, at the same time, they take their quite considerable accomplishments for granted. If I could just glance at this?"

# Chapter 3

ONCE THE MANUSCRIPT is firmly in my possession, cradled in my arms, I stand, ready to leave.

Spencer's mood seems to shift. He stands, too, insinuating himself between me and the door. "I'm not sure Ms., uh —" He casts around, searching for my name.

"Salter."

"I'm not sure this is the best way to proceed, Ms. Salter," he says urgently, his eyes glued to the manuscript.

"Nothing to worry about." I shrug off his concerns, sounding more confident than I feel.

"What I mean is, if I could just make a few more *minor* changes, I think the entire novel would benefit. There's a passage in chapter seventeen that could use more polishing." He moves closer. "If I could just have a day or two more."

I slide past him, hugging the bundle of paper tighter. "Mr. Stone, you're understandably a little nervous about handing your manuscript to someone new. I'm sure this is a fine piece of writing of the same calibre as your short fiction. I can't imagine it will require much work." I pat the substantial pile reassuringly. "I'll look this over on the weekend and phone you at 9:00 on Monday morning if I have any questions or concerns."

"Certainly," he says, through what seem to be gritted teeth.

I ease past him, nearly (but unfortunately not) dropping my new mug in the process. Never letting go of the manuscript, I slip out of the meeting room and into the front hall, Spencer close behind.

We stand in the doorway facing one another. For the space of a few seconds, Spencer remains frozen, as if uncertain what to do next. After a moment, he takes a deep breath that sounds almost like a sigh of resignation, then nods.

"Well, I commend the book to your no doubt very capable hands," he says, and gives me a tight little smile.

"Good."

"Yes," he says, but makes no move to depart.

"Well," I say, as he continues to stand rooted in the middle of the front hall. "If you'll excuse me," I wave vaguely in the direction of the office. "I really should be getting back to work."

He nods. "Yes, of course."

I turn and head down the hall. As the door into the office is about to swing shut behind me, I check over my shoulder. My last glimpse is of Spencer's dark figure loping down the front walk, away from the building.

Back at my desk I sit down and set the manuscript in front of me. I examine the file folder before me. It's satisfyingly weighty — *good, lots to work with,* I tell myself. I open it and find, taped to the inside of the folder, an envelope containing a computer disk. I pop the disk into my computer to see whether Spencer's using compatible software (it would make sense, but that's no guarantee) and an icon labelled "S&S" pops onto my screen. I double-click, and a series of files appears, labelled "ch. 01," "ch. 02" up to "ch. 30." This is a good sign.

I double-click on "ch. 17" and text appears on screen. Good, when the time comes, I'll be able to make changes and corrections onto the disk myself. That way I'll be able to hand the book to the designer on disk and she can transfer, or dump, the text into the page grid fast, clean, and with a minimum of errors. I'll print a hard copy of the final draft and hand hard copy and computer disk to Hill. Then, if further edits have to be made — and they will, Hill loves to tinker — all that will be required is a backspace here, a keystroke there, though changes can't be made without Spencer's okay.

But reading the manuscript on my monitor would give me a headache; I prefer to work from the hard copy. So I go back to the folder and begin at the beginning: first page, "Sound & Silence (working title)" — not bad, simple and elegant, although it sounds faintly familiar. I make a note to check whether there are any other books by that title in print. If that title's a go, I can work with it. Already I can visualize the cover: something uncomplicated, maybe just the title spelled out in a tasteful, classic typeface in a tasteful, classic colour on an ivory background, redolent of old parchment, giving the impression of timelessness, no image needed. Something to set it apart from the current fashion of dramatic, highly coloured covers, something that will broadcast the book's enduring, soon-to-be-a-classic excellence.

On to page two: "To Catherine, whose support has been unstinting." Well and good, Mrs. Stone acknowledged in print. A nice touch, classy — and does this mean the rumours I've heard about Spencer and a certain female (a poet/grad student, someone told me) are groundless?

Next, page three: a disclaimer of some sort. "This is a work of fiction. Any resemblance to persons living or dead is purely coincidental," etc., etc., etc. Yeah, fine, standard stuff; let's get down to business — where's the story? Page four, here we go: "It began in all innocence —" Oh, I like *that*, the reader's interest is piqued; already in those five simple words there are overtones of mystery, a hint of threat. Carry on.

My excitement is short-lived. By page ten a sort of dull confusion has set in. Something's wrong. Ostensibly a literary romance, there's a deadness to the writing; the restraint that works so well in Spencer's short stories, the flat, undramatic voice, doesn't work within the larger scale of a novel. It comes across as thin and whiny.

I flip to the end of the manuscript — 302 pages. Good, we've got space to manoeuvre: room to trim here, cut a bit there, pare the whole thing down, which will intensify the language, heighten the dramatic tension. At that length it won't be a massive book, but it will still be substantial, and if we play with type and page design — big margins and gutters, maybe bump the type to twelve point, increase the leading between the lines — we might be able to stretch it even longer.

So I go back to page ten and pick up where I left off, but by page fifty a mounting sense of horror overtakes me. This is awful; there's no story here, just a collection of characters walking (stiffly) in and out of unlikely situations, experiencing unlikely epiphanies and declaiming about them at length in unlikely and self-conscious language. No wonder Spencer didn't want to hand it over. He couldn't have done a better job parodying himself if he'd set out to do it deliberately.

And sentimental — the book is dripping with the kind of "I'll never again expose myself to the pain of love" mumbled-through-clenched-teeth sentimentality that I assumed went out the door with Hemingway. Allusions — the book positively bristles with references to the work of others: writers and poets, living and dead, none of them minor, as if by hitching his name to theirs, Spencer can pull himself up into their august company.

To be fair to him, I riffle through the stack of paper and read a couple of pages at random. Doesn't do anything for me. I take a stab at another section — still no suspension of disbelief.

Weak writing isn't the only difficulty; the narrative is problematic as well. The story charts the course of the ill-fated affair Sullivan, a university professor, pursues with a beautiful but ultimately unattainable graduate student. Could the story be autobiographical? No, I decide. After all, who would knowingly portray themselves so unflatteringly? The professor emerges as an emotional vampire incapable of real involvement with other people who takes up with students, messes around with their minds and relishes the resulting melodrama.

There are passages of lovely writing here and there, as good as anything Spencer has done before, but these passages, light and exquisite as meringue, are swamped by a sea of prose with the consistency of gloppy Jell-O.

Great, the novel that's supposed to bankroll Hunter Press for the next year is a dud. I've got to discuss this with Hill. If I had a month, there'd be an outside chance I could work with Spencer to produce a publishable novel — but a *week?* I'll tell Hill I'm not up to this. He may know a freelancer who could pull this off.

I'm halfway to his office when I hear a muffled groan from inside and see a pen fly across the doorway.

"Everything okay?" I call.

"No," Hill growls. "Just be glad I kept Kaz for myself and gave you Spencer."

This may not be the optimum time to share my insecurities. I return to my desk and reach for the phone. I have to get hold of Morris. Maybe he isn't gone for good — maybe he's just having a snit. Maybe he'll come back and take the millstone that is Spencer's novel from around my neck.

His line is busy. I replace the receiver and stare at the manuscript. In the best of all possible worlds, this pile of paper would be sitting on Hill's desk all tidied up and ready to go. In the next best of all possible worlds, it would be sitting on Morris's desk and it would be his responsibility. This must not be the best or even the next best of all possible worlds.

I check my watch and opt for the coward's way out — time for lunch. A quick phone call and it's all set. My friend Kayla will meet me for lunch at the Waterfront Café in ten minutes.

"Thank God you phoned," she says. "I was resigned to Stairmasters for lunch; now I can have calories."

"Off to lunch," I tell Jerri on the way out. "I'll be back in about an hour."

Behind her desk, Jerri signals to catch my attention. "What about Morris?" she calls in a loud whisper, her voice floating faintly down the hall after me.

Without looking back, I wiggle my fingers goodbye and make my getaway.

I could take the direct route to the restaurant, which would take me along the waterfront, but instead I choose the roundabout way, past the farmers' market where shiny Macintosh apples jostle against golden russets in the warm autumn sunlight, all in sight of city hall's great copper dome.

And now my guilty secret: standing at the corner of King and Brock streets, I glance across the street at the second-storey windows — I'm staring at Jim's apartment.

Is he there? My sixth sense says no. It used to be, when we were first involved — *in love,* let's be blunt — if I was at a party and he showed up, no matter where I was in the place, whether I could see him or not, when he showed up *I knew it.* It was eerie; the hair on the back of my neck would prickle, I'd turn around and there he'd be, just walking in the door.

"Oh, yeah." He laughed when I told him this once. "And I notice you have great luck with lotteries." But I could tell he was secretly flattered.

After we split up, I came to dread the tingling that told me he was present. I'd check the room the way a hunted animal checks for predators. When I located him, I did my best to avoid him.

Jim is a philosopher by avocation — we met while he was at university — and a house painter by vocation. This isn't as unusual as it might seem. I know two other PhDs in philosophy who are house painters. I'm not sure what the connection is; perhaps it's the fact that the job offers vast stretches of uninterrupted time to think, or perhaps it's the act of changing physical reality so easily — apply a coat of paint and, *voila,* a new house. Coupled with the fact there don't seem to be many openings for philosophers in the help-wanted section of the newspapers these days. Whatever his motivation, Jim makes a surprisingly good living painting houses and he seems to enjoy it.

We've been separated for three years and are in the process of divorcing. This town is small enough and our respective circles of friends are congruent enough that we encounter each other at parties and dinners fairly frequently. Acrimony has shifted into mutual tolerance.

He's a nice guy and sex was fine, so from time to time I lapse into self-pity and whine about how much I miss him. Em, ever the realist, has no patience for this sort of behaviour and keeps reminding me that *I* kicked *him* out. Which is true, but doesn't ease the pain.

I sort and fold through the memories the way I sort laundry. I enjoy folding laundry; there's comfort in how familiar these clothes are, how often I've handled this red check flannel shirt, worn blurry now by repeated washings, how many times I've shaken out this blue towel. To me, these are signs of continuity in a discontinuous life. That's what memory provides — a way to find meaning in this series of disjointed episodes we call life.

I sort through my laundry weekly; I sort through my memories at least as frequently, searching for patterns and clues to help me understand how I got where I am today.


Her name was Vivian. "Vivian the Plebeian," I called her. By conferring this nickname on her, I reduced her to a figure of ridicule. She was no longer the woman who had annihilated my marriage, she was a cartoon figure with a caption beneath her caricature.

Jim and Viv are ancient history now. Two months after their involvement became public — was *made* public by me at the top of my lungs at Chez Nous, the town's best French restaurant, where Jim and I had gone for a conciliatory supper that went wrong — Viv dumped Jim and moved in with Dan. To be fair, Viv has been democratic in her treatment of men; she left Dan for a second Jim, then Jim Two for Paul, and Paul for Konstant, her current partner. Paul lasted the longest — eight months.

How do I know all this? Try *not* knowing it in a town this size. I'd have to be a hermit to miss all the musical-chair pairings that go on. And since I am a bit of a recluse ("Sorry, I'll have to miss the party. Em has a school play on that night," "Oh, thanks for the invitation, but I'll be out of town at a book fair that weekend"), I have been known to stick my foot in it from time to time.

But in spite of my reclusive tendencies, I had heard about Jim and Sasha. I told Em that someone had told me that Sasha had changed her name to Astarte.

"A-who?" Em asked.

An ancient goddess, I explained. Em grimaced. I said that I'd heard that Sasha-now-Astarte was very nice, and wasn't Em fortunate to have met a deity. Em said Sasha wasn't as nice as me. I told her she was biased: we're programmed to prefer our own gene pool. That was when she informed me I had better taste in clothes than Astarte. How did she know? It turned out Em had met Astarte at lunch at Jim's the previous Sunday.

"Treacherous child, not to have mentioned it earlier," I teased.

"She was still Sasha then." Em grinned.

After the first episode with Vivian, I thought that Jim and I could work it out if we gave it another try. I almost managed to convince myself the affair was out of character for Jim. After all, we'd been together for seven years. One fling in that length of time didn't make me happy, but from information gleaned through reading and rumours, it actually seemed to fall below the statistical norm.

So we got a babysitter and went out to dinner a couple of times to talk things over. We poked and prodded at the relationship, looking for its weak points like a pair of dentists probing a sensitive tooth. Jim said he wanted sex more frequently, so we bought a calendar and made a schedule. I suggested we take a trip, so he went to a travel agency and returned laden with brochures and timetables. He pleaded boredom, so we sent away for a catalogue, which arrived in a brown paper wrapper, offering a selection of "sensual items." Certainly the pulp and paper industry benefited from the malaise we were experiencing.

All this optimism and fiddling, however, served only to prolong the death throes of our marriage. About a year after Vivian obtruded on our domestic conversation, my friend Kayla broke the news about Peggy.

I should have seen it coming. All of a sudden he got experimental in bed. Oh well, at least I could throw out all that lingerie and get back to flannel. I can't imagine a woman designed those teddies that snap at the crotch.

So why do I still eyeball his apartment? I've never examined this question thoroughly; there are areas of my psyche I avoid the way one avoids the San Andreas fault in earthquake season. But the truth is, I suspect I still harbour a weakness for Jim. Weakness is exactly what it is, too. My bedraggled dictionary, its red cover torn, the pages worn soft and dog-eared with use, defines weakness as: "1. the state or quality of being weak. 2. a defect or weak point: fault. 3. a penchant or fondness with *for; a weakness* for pastry." Definitions two and three pretty well cover it. My feelings for Jim run like fault lines through my life *and* I have a weakness not only for pastry but for him — despite the fact that I can eradicate the consequences of pastry more quickly than I can deal with the bruises he inflicts on my psyche. I eat a doughnut, I hit the rowing machine for an hour. On the other hand, I talk to Jim on the phone ("Change of plans — I can't take Em this weekend") and I'm rigid with anger for days afterward.


These are the thoughts that occupy me as I walk to the Waterfront Café to meet Kayla. Today she's all bubbly and excited. The Café is a chic, dark restaurant of shining surfaces, muted music, and minimalist entrees — a sliver of chicken, two slices of zucchini, an ice cream scoop-sized serving of rice, and a sprig of cilantro artfully arranged on a white plate and decorated with a dusting of paprika in the pattern of a snowflake.

Kayla is my best friend — even when she talks straight to me about Jim, I love her. She's a real-estate agent, and in a town full of tasteful pearl necklaces and tweed outfits, she wears big jewellery and bright colours. She's probably what keeps me sane these days.

"Elaine, I saw the cutest place this morning. The moment I walked in, I thought of you —"

"Kayla," I interrupt. "I'm not buying a place. I can't afford it."

"What are you talking about? You're going to get a settlement from Jim, you'll buy a house. It's not just you; there's Em to think of, too. You don't want to keep dragging the poor child from place to place. She needs *roots*." At this point, she *tings* her fork against the side of her plate for emphasis.

I glower at her across the table. Pulling Em into this is dirty pool. "I am not 'dragging her from place to place,' as you put it. We've only moved twice in three years, and we've been where we are now for two years. And who knows if I'll get a settlement. He doesn't even answer his phone. I haven't talked to him in a week. Half the time when I leave a message, he never gets back to me."

"Get your lawyer to send his lawyer a letter," she says matter-of-factly.

"I don't *want* to. I don't want the situation to escalate. I want to work this out like grown-ups."

"Only one of you is a grown-up."

"Oh, come on, Kayla, Jim's a grown-up."

"Only in chronological terms. You know, Jim doesn't really exist," she says. "There's a guy out there walking around named Jim with all the physical attributes of the Jim you're always talking about, but all this stuff he does to you is just things you're doing to punish yourself. Really. Otherwise you'd say, 'Grow up, Jim, and get with the program. Let's settle this whole thing so we can get on with life.' I mean," Kayla continues, "you need to examine why you feel compelled to punish yourself like this."

When she talks about Jim this way, I'm convinced she spent too much time in California during her youth. (She admits to having lived there a couple of years; I suspect it was much longer.) On the other hand, she's survived two divorces and is flourishing, so maybe there's something to what she says.

How Kayla and I met: I don't know what possessed Jim and me back then; for a brief moment we deluded ourselves into believing we could afford a house. Between my salary and the salary Jim anticipated earning once he finished his degree and got a tenure-track job, we really thought we could own a home. I imagine it was a relatively standard set of hallucinations Jim and I shared, delusions common to other people in our age and income bracket: him, me and Em eating breakfast in a sun-drenched kitchen; the three of us curling up on the couch in front of the TV on those cold winter nights; a room for Em where she could write on the walls with crayons; a bathroom on the same floor as our bedroom — at that time we were living on the second and third floors of a duplex and stumbling down and up stairs in the middle of the night. Maybe another addition to the family. Even the thought of paying municipal taxes — roll numbers and mill rates — was attractive, a rite of passage into adulthood.

So I'd scoured the real-estate section of the newspaper, searching for the house of our dreams. When I found one that looked likely, I phoned the real-estate company. The next day, Kayla drove her sporty little red car into my life, her purple scarves fluttering.

Later she told me that that first day she thought I had a poker up my ass, I was *so* proper, so *haute WASP.* I, on the other hand, was immediately charmed, fascinated and relieved. Finally, here was someone who said what she thought, straight-up, no window-dressing. She told me the place we'd been looking at wasn't right for us. The location was wrong and it was too small.

She laughed when I reminded her later about that first meeting. She had been trying to tell me that the house was a shitbox but she hadn't wanted to use such colourful language until she knew me better. "Nightmare" was a more accurate description of the place. The house came complete with sagging ceilings, bulging walls and dark, dingy, box-like rooms.

As it developed, the perfect house never materialized. Shortly after Kayla and I visited the nightmare house, the Jim and Viv Event occurred, and my life shifted gears dramatically.

Instead of getting a house, I got Kayla as a friend — much the better deal. She's low-maintenance; there are no fluctuating interest rates to cause mortgage-payment anxiety, no escalating property taxes, no leaking ceilings when it rains, no sidewalks to shovel in winter. And I don't have to spend twenty years whittling away at the principal until I know it belongs to me; I already know Kayla's affection is mine.

It's her affection and support I count on at times like this, when the going gets tough. "I don't want to talk about Jim anymore," I say. "I want to talk about my eventful morning. For one thing, I've been promoted to Senior Editor."

"That's terrific," she says. "Congratulations. Let's celebrate." After a moment's pause. "What happened to Morris?"

"That's my other news," I say, and tell her about Morris's meltdown and Spencer's book. "I think it's supposed to be a literary romance, although you could have fooled me. It's more like an anti-romance or a deconstructo-romance. My job is to edit it, make it publishable in one week. I have no idea how I'm going to pull that off."

"I thought you were working on *Highways and Byways.*"

"We sent it off to the printers yesterday."

She shrugs. "So tell Hill that Spencer's book is garbage."

"I think that's my option of last resort." I explain about Hunter's precarious financial situation, how Hill is trying to salvage Kaz's book. "I don't think he could manage Spencer's, too. And if I don't manage Spencer, I'll probably be out of a job."

For a moment she's silent, then she says, "Revise it yourself."

The simplicity of this knocks the wind out of me. "What do you mean?" I ask.

"You've been putting books together for ages now. You have the story. You tell me some of the writing's good. All you have to do is cut the bad parts and tie the good parts together so it all works, right?" Kayla shrugs. "I mean, I'm in real estate, so what do I know, but it seems pretty straightforward to me."

"It's not ethical."

"It's not ethical to dedicate a book to your wife while you're making whoopee with some cute little poet, is it?"

"You know about the poet?" I ask.

"Of course."

"How?"

"I have my sources," she says airily.

"I should have known. It's a good thing I have no life to speak of," I tell her. "Or what news would you be spreading about me?" I turn my mind back to the matter at hand. "I don't know." But I do know — she's right. I *could* do it. It wouldn't be too difficult. The structure's in place. Like an armature inside a clay sculpture, the bones of the plot are there, buried under a pile of verbiage. The story's somewhat unlikely, but there's nothing a little tinkering can't fix. He's got enough bits of good writing that just need to be strung together well.

The conviction grows in me that Kayla may be correct. Although I've never put a novel together this way, I did organize that book of essays in six weeks last year, and I've just spent a month improving the travel guide. So I have the technology, and the systems are in place.

Already I'm in editor mode, working the schedule out in my head, figuring backwards from the November publication date. It would be tight, but I could do it. And what have I got to lose? If it works and the book sells, the press will be solvent and I'll probably continue to have a job; if I don't do it, there's no way on earth the book will sell and Hunter Press will be down the tubes.

For a moment the situation looks brighter, then I remember Spencer. He might not be happy to have his book hijacked this way. "Spencer may object," I point out.

"What about your friend Paige?" Kayla says. "You tell me she's a force to be reckoned with in the publishing world — knows all, sees all. Get hold of her; ask her if she has any suggestions."

Paige. Paige is perfect. Because of her position at *City* magazine, she has a certain amount of power in literary circles. She is wooed by publicists, invited to glitterati events. She circulates, she knows everyone. She has clout — she might even have clout with Spencer.

# *Chapter 4*

THE FIRST THING TO DO, I decide when I get back to the office, is finish reading Spencer's manuscript all the way through. I've just settled at my desk, ready to dive in, when the phone buzzes.

"Hi, it's Jerri."

"Hi, Jerri." I wait for some follow-up. When none is forthcoming, I say, "Can I help you?"

"Oh, right. There's a call for you on — wait a minute." I wait while she gives the matter some thought. There is only one line lit up. "Line one," she finally says.

"Thanks, Jerri. And can you hold my calls for the rest of the day, please?"

"'Kay."

"Jerri? Do you know who's on the line?" But she's gone.

I punch the blinking light and say in my most professional voice, "Elaine Salter."

"Hello, Elaine; it's your mother."

I knew that. I knew from the first word. No one else can so successfully invest one sentence — a mere five words — with such a guilt-inducing inflection. "Hello, Mother."

"Don't sound so happy to hear from me. I can tell you can barely contain yourself."

"I just had a big problem handed to me. I'm a bit stressed."

"Stress is life's way of telling you you're not dead yet."

"Yeah, thanks."

"Listen, I won't keep you. Ed and I are coming to town tomorrow. He's got something going on. Ed?" I hear her call. "What's going on?" A distant, mumbled reply. "Reunion," she reports back to me. "University. What engineers have to talk about, who knows? Anyway, we'll be in town for a few days."

"Mother, I'm really busy."

"Who says it's you we want to see? I want to see my gorgeous granddaughter. We won't bother you. You won't even know we're there."

*Yeah, sure.*

"But we want to take Emily and you to dinner tomorrow. At 5:30, usual place."

"I'm really busy, Mother."

A sigh. "I was hoping to surprise you, Elaine, but you always manage to make things difficult. In case you've forgotten, it's your birthday tomorrow. So you can spare half an hour from your busy life and let your mother — who gave birth to you, may I remind you — take you out to dinner. It's not like I ask a lot from you, and I promise we won't keep you. It'll be just hello, goodbye and a nice meal." I hear a click; our conversation is over.

Oh, great. Birthday dinner. I sit staring at the receiver. Typical, just typical. Do I phone her back and beg off? That's asking for a fight, which I have no energy for right now. No, maybe by tomorrow my luck will change and I'll have stomach flu or salmonella or something contagious. Maybe by then I can come up with a reasonable excuse.

I replace the receiver, and a moment later the phone buzzes again. I pick up expecting Jerri and instead find myself talking to someone from the printers about the *Highways and Byways* schedule. We crunch numbers for ten minutes, and when I finish that conversation, Jerri puts through yet another call.

If I were paranoid, I'd think Jerri was actively trying to sabotage me, but I don't think she's that strategic. These interruptions are the result of her bubble-brain nature.

Instead of picking up, I walk over to Jerri's desk. She's counting copies of *Spoonerisms,* our most recent cookbook, into a box for shipping.

"Jerri," I say, leaning against the door frame. "Would you hold my calls this afternoon, please? Hill just handed me a huge project and I really can't talk to anyone. If it's Em or her school, I'll talk to them. Otherwise, could you take messages?"

She has begun wrapping packing tape around the box. Every time she pulls the tape dispenser, there's a loud shriek as the tape pulls off the roll. "What?" She looks up. "Oh, sorry. Sure, yeah I will." She sets down the tape and leans toward me. Glancing in the direction of Hill's office, she says in a low voice, "What about Morris? What happened?"

I'm not certain how much to tell her. "I don't know. He lost it at the production meeting this morning and stormed out."

"Oh." Jerri nods. I note a flicker of interest in her eyes. "Is he coming back?"

"Without a doubt," I tell her, trying to make myself believe my own words.

I return to my desk. Five minutes later the phone buzzes. "Jerri," I call. "Can you take a message?"

"Oh right, sorry."

It's clear I won't have any peace here, so I decide to pack up and go home, where I'll be able to read without interruption. I lean in Hill's office. "I'm taking Spencer's manuscript home. I can't work here right now — it's a zoo."

"Fine," he says without looking up, slashing at the paper in front of him with a pen.

On the way out I lean over Jerri's desk. "Can I book the conference room for next week?" This will be the best place to work with Spencer.

"No can do," Jerri tells me brightly. "Hill's already booked it."

"For the whole week?"

"Yup. Something about finishing the book before it finishes him."

"Ah." Exactly how I feel. "I'm going home now. I'll be there in twenty minutes." With the answering machine on, I add silently. That way I can screen my calls. "If anyone calls, just give them my number, please."

"Sure."

"And thanks again for the birthday present, Jerri. It was very kind of you."

"Have a good one," she calls after me.

Em's asked me to pick her up some shampoo, so on my way home I nip into the drugstore and buy a few things. Shopping bags, purse and briefcase in hand, I negotiate the crowds of people thronging the sidewalks on this sunny autumn afternoon. I've waddled halfway up Princess Street before it occurs to me that I haven't read anything Spencer has written recently. This will not do. If I hope to understand the man's style, I'll have to familiarize myself with his more recent work. Not a happy thought, but it can't be avoided. Damn — I should have nicked some copies from the office before I left. We always have a few of everything sitting around to send out for reviews and promotional activities.

I stop stock-still in the middle of the sidewalk; a man following in my wake collides with me and we exchange imprecations. *Where?* I ask myself. *The library?* Possibly, but I'd really like my own copies so I can annotate as I go, marking good passages and characteristic turns of phrase. Now I'll be reduced to actually buying some of his books and increasing his royalties. *Where?*

Then I remember, further along, tucked into a narrow old dingy building, is a second-hand bookstore I've walked past many times but never gone into. Possibly I'll be able to find used copies of Spencer's books there.

I resume my progress westward until I come to the store. A faded sign in gothic lettering — black script on a pale blue background — swings over the door, *Palimpsest Books.* Nice name. There's a moment's drama when my bags and I get stuck in the doorway, but a sharp shove, judiciously applied, breaks the gridlock and I stumble inside.

After the bright sunshine outside, it takes my eyes a while to adjust to the store's murky interior. I stand blinking for a few seconds while shelves crowded with hundreds of books swim slowly into focus. The smell of the place brings to mind summer cottages: the aromas of dust and mildew.

Now that I can see more clearly, the sheer number of books packed into the rather limited space available is overwhelming. Every horizontal surface is jammed with volumes of all shapes and sizes — paperbacks, coffee table books, texts. *How am I going to find anything in here?*

At that moment, a subtle noise alerts me to someone's presence. I turn quickly and notice for the first time a counter behind me, to the right of the entrance, hidden beneath piles of books and magazines. Behind the counter is the person who cleared his throat.

*Those would be hooded eyes,* I'm surprised to realize. I've read about them before but have never encountered any in real life. Well, there they are, set in a not-too-bad looking face. A bit weathered, friendly, and in the hooded eyes I detect flashes of irony. The man has medium length medium brown hair and a medium build. Although taller than me, he's considerably shorter than Jim. Offhand I'd guess he's in his early forties. There is a comfortable, lived-in quality to him — the edges have been knocked off a little.

"May I help you?" His voice is quiet and laconic.

"I'm looking for books by Spencer Stone. Can you point me in the right direction?"

"Spencer Stone," he repeats thoughtfully. "Which titles?"

"Oh, anything you've got that's recent."

"Just a moment. Excuse me." His manner is measured, somewhat formal. He disappears up a small flight of stairs tucked behind a shelf of books that I hadn't noticed before. In a few moments he emerges with a handful of trade paperbacks. "Here we are," he announces.

I drop my bags and run a finger down the pile of spines. (There's something pleasantly macabre about the anatomical terms we use to describe the parts of books.) *Point and Counterpoint, Lost Harmonic, Song in Shadow:* yup, yup, yup.

"Dandy. I'll take them."

He begins to tally up the total while I scrabble through my purse looking for my wallet. *Damn, I've spent all my cash at the drugstore.* "Will you take a cheque?"

"Certainly. The total is $26.75."

I fill it out. "Do you need any identification?"

"You're with Hunter Press, aren't you?" he asks.

"How do you know?" The words jump out sharply. *Earth to Elaine — tone it down, or you're going to sound like a real bitch.*

He gestures at the books all around us. "We're in the same business, just at different ends of it. You're at the production end, I'm at the supply end. We're both losing market share to videos, DVDs and CD-ROMs." He smiles wryly. "I've been to a few Hunter Press book launches. The food's adequate, but whoever selects the wine should be shot."

*I hate when this happens.* I live my life as if no one's looking — scurrying up the street looking like a bag lady, heading off to work wearing mismatched socks, tearing around town in my rustbucket of a car, always assuming I might as well be invisible — only to discover people are watching all the time. When will I learn?

"I don't remember seeing you at any of the launches." *Does that sound paranoid, or what?*

"Oh, I keep a low profile. I just pop in for a few minutes early in the evening. I have to get home before the babysitter burns out."

*Babysitter? What about Mom? Where is she?* This is one of those moments that throws into relief how very different the current world is from the world of my childhood. In those days, everyone had a mom. Mine lurked on the other side of my bedroom door when friends came over and always managed to pop in with an offer of milk and cookies just when the conversation was getting interesting. She drove me to piano class after school and knew how I spent every moment of my spare time.

These days the possibilities are rife: maybe Mom left and Dad has sole custody; maybe they share custody and Dad has the kids every other week; perhaps Mom works nights; or it could be Dad lives with another Dad and Mom lives with another Mom — the permutations are dizzying. And, of course, since I'm a liberal, tolerant product of Western civilization, which has just turned the corner from one millennium to the next, I don't ask where Mom is. I merely smile and say, "You have kids?"

"Just one. An eleven year old boy. The babysitter's good for about two hours, but by then Isaac's worn her to a frazzle. So I make sure I'm home by 9:00 to get him to bed."

"I understand that in a few years you'll probably have to drag him *out* of bed each morning."

"So I hear," he says. "Out of curiosity, why Spencer Stone?"

"Oh, I'm editing his novel. I need to get a feel for his writing."

The ghost of a smile flits across his face. "The mysterious, much-rumoured novel. I've heard about it. I look forward to reading the work in its entirety someday. Have you known Spencer long?"

Do I detect a sudden sharpness in his tone? "No." I shake my head. "I met him for the second time today. Morris, the other editor, was working with him, but Morris is, uh, on sabbatical."

"Ah." He nods. "But haven't you read these?" He indicates the pile of books. "Hunter Press publishes him."

I shrug. "Oh, I just need to refresh my memory," I reply vaguely, distracted by the dialogue going on in my head. *Should I? Can I? I'll feel like a fool. What is there to lose? He's interesting to talk to, no stranger to books, he has a kid — grist for the conversational mill when all else runs dry. Why not?* "I'm sorry, I don't know your name."

"Nathan." He holds out his hand. "Nathan Marks."

"Elaine Salter." I shake his hand. "Oh, of course, my name's on my cheque." Flustered, I gather up my various bags and packages, stashing the books with a package of tampons. "Nice to meet you."

"Good luck with the novel," he says, holding the door as I ease my way out. Do I detect a hint of laughter in his voice, a flicker of amusement in his eyes? *It might be nice to get to know him,* the idea flashes through my mind like a shooting star. *It's been a while.* A table in a darkened corner of some restaurant, a half-empty carafe of wine, a murmur of conversation, a shimmer of laughter — for an instant I can see it clearly, then reality intrudes. No time to stop and pursue the possibilities now — I've got to deal with Spencer's book. I've got momentum, I'm in motion with this load. If I stop before I get home, I may never get started again.

# Chapter 5

HOME AT LAST, I STUMBLE INSIDE and set down the shopping bags and briefcase in the middle of the chaos that predominates in my entryway hall. I stand for a moment and take a deep breath, running down my mental list for the evening: get this stuff put away, change clothes, pick up Em —

*Em.* Oh, Lord, what am I going to do about Em while I'm working on the book? Tomorrow's an early dismissal day. She'd be perfectly happy to vegetate in front of the TV all weekend, but that's not an option. I need long, uninterrupted expanses of time to get this finished. If Em's around, we'll end up chatting and goofing around.

Check the clock: 2:00, school's out in an hour and a half. On Thursdays she goes to the after-school program until I pick her up on my way home from work, usually around 5:15. I have three hours to get something organized.

*Jim.* If I manage to reach him, he'll probably try to weasel out of it, but this is an emergency and God knows I've covered for him enough. Last winter, for example, so he could go on a skiing weekend. "Please, Elaine. I'll cover for you sometime." I could hear the edge of desperation in his voice, the I-might-get-lucky undercurrent of excitement. I could sympathize. It had been a long time since I'd gotten lucky.

"Okay, but you owe me."

"Fine, fine, fine." His relief was palpable.

I hit the speed-dial button for Jim's number. He's probably at work. I'll likely get his answering machine. Telephone tag. If he doesn't call me back, I'll have to try one of Em's friends' moms.

"Hello?" a familiar deep voice says.

Expecting a machine, I am speechless for an instant. "Jim. Why aren't you out painting houses?"

There's a moment's silence. "Hello, Elaine," Jim says coolly.

"Hi, Jim."

"How are you?" His tone is resolutely even. I can imagine the expression on his face: quizzical, closed-off, not giving anything away.

"That's why I'm calling. Remember what's-her-name — the ski bunny?" The instant the words are out, it occurs to me this may not be the best way to go about asking for a favour — reminding him of failed relationships. I happen to know that that one went downhill — metaphorically speaking — pretty quickly. Being reminded of her may not predispose him to helping me now.

Patiently, like a parent talking to a demanding child, he says, "Her name was Kim."

"Remember how you said you owed me?"

Another pause. "Why?"

I recall this sparring, this back and forth, from when we were married. Neither one giving an inch. These days our conversations are full of echoes.

"I'm calling you on it. I've got to work this weekend, and I need you to take Em tonight until next Thursday."

"Work?" he says, his voice tinged with doubt.

"Work." I give him a brief summary of the day's events. "So I have to sit at my desk all day, all week and try to drag a novel out of the manuscript from hell I just got handed. And I'll have to track down Spencer, too, and persuade him, somehow, to co-operate."

"Really?" He sounds unconvinced.

"Jim, it's legit," I say. "Don't make me jump through hoops about this. When you asked, I covered for you."

"Yeah, you did," he allows.

"Did you get lucky?" I blurt. *Oh, God, how did that get out?*

Rueful laughter. "No, I didn't. She was into romance — flowers, poetry —"

"Taking baths by candlelight?" I read women's magazines now and then in the grocery store check-out line; I'm up on all the current trends: aromatherapy, power yoga, candlelit baths.

"You know," he says in a bemused tone, "I got wax spilled all over my chest. I tried pulling it out of my chest hair. Hurt like hell. I finally had to cut a whole clump of hair out. Anyway, she wanted more —" He hesitates, searching for words.

"Verbal foreplay?"

"That'll do," he replies. "It was as if I was supposed to put on some kind of performance. I was tired. I just wasn't up for it."

"Figuratively speaking," I say.

Jim laughs again, sounding more relaxed and friendly. "Not in any respect." Then he adds, "No, I didn't get lucky."

"I'm sorry."

"You win some —"

"You lose some," I finish. "So, can you take Em?"

"Sure."

"Today you'll need to pick her up at 5:15, 5:30. Tomorrow's a half day at school, so you'll need to pick her up at noon."

"No problem."

"She's got a toothbrush at your place, right? I can just phone the school and tell them you'll be picking her up this afternoon, okay?"

"Sure," he says.

"Make sure she eats her veg. Don't forget to brush her hair. She can't do it by herself. She shouldn't watch any scary movies because they give her nightmares, and she should be in bed by 9:00."

"Relax, Elaine. She's my daughter, too. I know all this stuff. It's not like I'm not on the scene."

Chastened, I say, "You're right. I'm sorry. Thanks, Jim."

So many of my responses to Emily are determined by my relationship with my mother. I remember holding Em when she was just born and thinking, *I promise I won't do to you what my mother did to me. I won't make those mistakes.* A rash promise, but accurate in one respect: I didn't make all the mistakes my mother made, I made a whole set of different, new ones. Because I was sent to bed at 8:30 every night until I was twelve years old, Em wasn't going to have a set bedtime — until exhaustion forced me to impose one, and by then 8:30 looked pretty good. We fought that one out for at least six months and compromised on 9:00.

In any situation, I'd examine how my mother had handled it, and then take the opposite tack — until I realized I am not my mother, and Emily isn't me. I am thankful the child has a good, sensible head on her shoulders (God only knows which side of the family she gets it from; Jim's family is as idiosyncratic in its own way as mine) and seems to have emerged from the whole experience relatively unscathed.

I know my anxieties often have no basis in reality, or if they do — so what? She could get hit by a bus while walking to school; the debris from an obsolete weather satellite might come crashing through the atmosphere and crush her while she's playing in the park; she could have an embolism — there are any number of bad things that could happen to her, all of them beyond my control.

Back to the matter at hand. I've got to get past the touch of resentment I sense in Jim's voice. He thinks I'm critical of his parenting, but I'm not. It's only my anxiety talking. I know — change tack. I'll show him how well we get along, what good friends we are by asking about his current squeeze in a casual, non-confrontational manner. "How's Sa — Astarte?" I ask about Jim's current love interest.

Silence.

At my end of the phone line, I wince. *Oops. I must have put my foot in it again.*

"It'll just be Em and me, okay, Elaine?" I've known him long enough to understand the edge to his voice means: *Mind your own business. She's not on the scene anymore and I'm miserable and want to get away. I wish I could tell you all about it, but I can't because guys don't talk about that stuff and I'd be thinking you'd be thinking, "Couldn't you tell the woman was a flake?"* Or something along those lines.

"Fine." Which means: *Fine, and I'm sorry if you're unhappy.* But he probably hears only *fine.* "Can you get Em to phone me before she goes to bed?"

"*Relax,* Elaine."


I return to the pile of bags and parcels sitting on the floor and dig through it until I unearth my briefcase and the bag of books from

Palimpsest. Fire up the coffee maker and I'm off to my aerie. That's how I think of my office up on the third floor. Dusty, dark, but my own.

First things first: another call to Morris. No luck there, only the phone, ringing and ringing into the unanswering void. Next I've got to track down Spencer and nail down a meeting on Monday. I'll try the university.

"Department of English," a pleasant young woman answers.

"Hello, this is Elaine Salter from Hunter Press. I'm trying to contact Professor Stone. I'm working on his manuscript and I have some questions. It's rather urgent."

"Professor Stone isn't in at the moment. May I take a message, or would you like his voice mail?"

"If I could leave my name and phone number with you, that would be great." Voice mail is easily ignored; a message from a real live human being is less easy to disregard. "Is he gone for the day?"

"I believe he's in a meeting."

I leave my name, number and a message that is explicit in indicating how pressing the situation is but vague about what the precise nature of the problem is, then hang up and take a deep breath. Time to assess the project.

I can sit here and wait for Spencer to get back to me, but that may take a while. In a meeting on a Thursday afternoon? Possibly. Or she may be covering for him. He may be composing a couplet or two with the poet. *Cynic,* I chastise myself. But the question is, what next? Sit and wait, or get on with it?

Why not make a start — give the manuscript a quick once-over to see what works, what doesn't, which changes can be made without Spencer's help and which ones I'll have to consult him about?

First I need to find a clean spot on which to work. Just shove all this paperwork to one side, then deposit the manuscript et al on my desk — a jerry-built contraption constructed from a door supported by sawhorses at both ends. Boot up my trusty computer and try to find my chair — oh, here it is, hidden under magazines (articles I will read any day now), solicitations for charitable contributions (eyes, liver, kidneys and other organs entreat me to send money) and unsolicited manuscripts (there may be a diamond in the rough waiting to be discovered).

What I know about Spencer I have picked up from the sort of free-floating talk that circulates in a small town. This talk can be at once vaguely noncommittal and brutally vicious. No one is ever willing to be identified as the source of any of it; such rumours as float around are always ascribed to someone else, usually a nebulous someone: "An editor I know at Brand X publishing house ...," "A friend of mine who works for the university ..." You can avoid listening to the rumours, but most people don't.

Opinions about Spencer seem to fall into two camps. Members of the first camp feel he's a fine writer who has a few quirks, but who doesn't? Those in the other camp hold the position he's a know-nothing opportunist who produced a few competent stories a decade ago, has merely repeated himself since, and trades on his connections and the strength of past achievements. As I say, such talk can be brutal. I don't go in search of this information, I just hear it in passing and file it in my memory banks.

I do know that earlier this year Spencer returned from a semester's residence at a university on the West Coast and is slated to headline a writers' festival in Toronto next spring. (One of our poets is on the bill, too. When I asked whether she'd consider travelling down with Spencer and taking her own books, saving us shipping costs in the process, her answer was swift and emphatic — no.)

Plus there is the buzz about his dalliances. Rumour has it that before the poet, there was a translator, and before that a research assistant. Rumour never mentions his wife.

But none of this is pertinent now. What matters now is to whip this manuscript into something resembling shape. I work my way from start to finish, making notes as I go. It's hard work keeping track of plots and subplots and all the characters who come and go. I get up and reheat my cup of coffee several times.

As I read, understanding dawns. A while ago — years ago, probably — Spencer began a novel. My guess is that initially it came fairly quickly and without too much effort, the story flowing out of his pen, word following speedily on word, phrase building on phrase in swift succession. I can discern, beneath obscuring layers of subsequent writing, the outline of a fairly straightforward story.

Over time, though, something happened. Maybe after the success of the first collection of short stories he began to take himself seriously, to try complicated and ambitious things. Maybe he read too many reviews of his stories and lost the shape of what he wanted to tell. Perhaps writing got tangled up with all sorts of other stuff: literary theories, cachet, friendships. And then the words dried up — Spencer choked.

Casting about in an effort to continue writing something — anything — he added layer on layer of text. Now Spencer's much-touted muscular prose lies buried beneath a slag heap of unnecessary writing. The challenge will be to excavate the worthwhile stuff from that morass. Is there enough good material to tie into a cohesive novel? For now, all I can do is push ahead and hope. I'd love to dive into the manuscript, tear it apart and put it back together in a more workable fashion — but I can't do that without first discussing it with Spencer.

It's clear now why Spencer was dragging his feet about handing the manuscript over to Morris and why he seemed so anxious when I blithely scooped it up. (It's amazing what you can accomplish sometimes when you don't know what you're doing.) On some level he must know how much more work the novel needs before it will be ready for publication — not a simple edit, something closer to a complete rewrite.

So why was he lugging the manuscript around in the first place, why has he even agreed to let Hill publish it? My guess is, despite his successes in that area, short stories don't cut it in Spencer's estimation. To be a "real" writer, you have to have a novel under your belt — the longer the better (a typical male sentiment regarding things below the belt). So for over ten years, he's been toting this manuscript around as proof to himself and others he's a real writer, a serious writer, hard at work on an important, *long* novel. And when Hill finally cornered him, Spencer either didn't have the cojones to tell the truth about the novel or he secretly hoped the book isn't as bad as he suspects it is. It is, in fact, as bad, and may be even worse.

When, after a couple of hours, I realize I've reread the same sentence five times without understanding what's being said, I decide it's time to break for food. All the caffeine is setting up cerebral static and making my brain hum.

Opening the refrigerator at this point in the week is problematic. Em and I usually go shopping on Saturday, so by Thursday the cupboard is often nearly bare. I'm in luck — the remains of an eggplant parmigiana from Tuesday night's dinner, and a couple of single-serving yogurts.

I settle down to eat, wondering whether I should call Kayla later, when the phone rings. Emily — my heart jumps to my throat: probably some disaster has occurred and there's a policeman on the other end of the line with dire news. "Yes?"

"Elaine Salter?"

"Yes."

"This is Nathan Marks."

Nathan Marks? Oh, right — the used-book man. "Yes?" Curiosity mingled with suspicion — why is he phoning?

"I'm sorry to bother you at home. After you left the store I found another book with some stories by Spencer Stone in it."

"Yes?"

"If you like, I can hold it here at the store for you. Or I could drop it off this evening on my way home. You're on the way."

A moment's panic: *how does he know where I live?* Then I remember my cheque; my address is on it.

"I wouldn't want to inconvenience you —"

"Not at all." There's that formal, slightly ironic tone again. "I don't live too far from you. On the other hand," he pauses for a beat, "if you'd rather I didn't —"

"It's very kind of you. What time would you be heading home?"

"Six, quarter past."

"Well, sure, thank you."

So much for vast, uninterrupted expanses of time. Now, do I rush downstairs, take a shower, change into something a bit more flattering and get my hair together, or do I go with nature? Em would scoff, *This isn't a date, Mom. The guy's just dropping something off — don't have a cow.* My mother would say, *It can't hurt. If God wanted us to look natural, why did He invent makeup? You want nature, look at the Grand Canyon. Is that what you want to look like? Wear a little lipstick, at least.* I decide to stick with nature. I rarely wear lipstick to edit a book.

Do I offer him something to eat? A drink? All I have is half a bottle of white left over from last month's launch, and I know his opinion of Hunter Press's wine selection.

I'm too old for this. I can't deal with the anxiety. The last time I went on a date, I broke out in hives. Take deep breaths — one, two, three. Check my watch: I've got a while to go before he's due to show up. Good, maybe I can plough through a few more chapters.

Two cups of coffee later and deep into a passage concerning a tertiary character, I almost don't hear the doorbell ringing. I'm trying to figure out how to excise the character and retain some of the dazzling writing when the sound finally registers.

I rush down the two flights of stairs and open the door just as Nathan's about to turn and walk away. He's standing in what I refer to as the courtyard, a section of shabby alleyway running along the west side of the building that serves as my yard.

"Sorry," I say breathlessly, "I was working up on the third floor. Come in. Please."

A quick glance over my left shoulder: the scene registers as if I'm seeing the place for the first time. *Oh, Lord, what a mess.* Em's bike stands propped against the far wall, mine leans against hers; our coats, hats and sweaters lie in a jumble on the sofa to the right of the entrance; a couple of baskets of laundry, the clothes in various stages of being folded, are stashed in one corner; and firewood, once stacked in an orderly fashion, now sits in a tumbled pile beside the woodstove.

Nathan shakes his head. "I can't stay. I've got to rescue the babysitter from Isaac. If I don't get home and feed him supper before his blood sugar plummets, he's hell on wheels for the rest of the night."

*Oh, sure,* I think. *Good excuse. Hide behind your kid — I recognize the manoeuvre, use it all the time myself. I've scared him off with all this mess,* I wail to myself. *He probably thinks I'm a slob.* It's not always like this, I want to tell him. Mother may have been right — a little housecleaning never hurt anyone.

He pulls a book from his jacket pocket and hands it to me. "This includes Spencer's earliest efforts." He holds out a slender volume, its pale grey cover worn and stained.

"You're sure you can't come in?" I take the proffered book and wave it in the general direction of the building's interior. "A cup of coffee?" *Am I being too forward? Do I sound desperate?*

"No, no." He smiles. "I can't risk antagonizing the babysitter. She's the first one Isaac's liked in a long time, and she doesn't have a boyfriend yet."

*I've gone too far. He thinks I'm pushy.* "How much?" I ask, waving the book.

Nathan shakes his head. "Think of it as my contribution to literature in this country."

"Thanks." *Game over. I've blown it again. Why can't I keep my house clean and my mouth shut?*

He's turning, about to leave, when he pauses. "We could go for coffee sometime."

"Sure." *Maybe there's hope after all. Whose move is it now, his or mine? I'm out of practice, I don't know what the rules are anymore. Get real. He's just being nice. He doesn't really mean it. It's one of those vague statements designed to get him out of an unpleasant situation without letting me down too hard.*

"I'll set something up with the babysitter and give you a call, okay?"

*Maybe he means it.* "Great." *Did that sound sarcastic?* "Yeah, give me a call." *Was that too eager?* "Whenever's good for you. My schedule's pretty flexible." *Stop babbling.*

"All right." He's gone.

*He'll never phone. He was just being friendly. Look at this place.* I close the door and kick a stray boot across the floor. Who in their right mind would get involved with someone who lives like this? Should I clean up? Can't — got to get this manuscript edited. I'll get to it later. Although, come to think of it, isn't that what I told myself last time?

I stand leaning against the closed door, staring at the book in my hand. It's an anthology of short stories. I flip to the table of contents: two entries by Spencer. I carry it back up to the third floor and settle among the piles of books and papers and analyze the situation. To get this job finished, I'll have to be systematic or I haven't a hope.

I check the clock: 6:29 and no phone call yet from Spencer. Maybe the secretary missed him, or maybe he got the message and is going to phone me later, or maybe he's avoiding me. I just hope I won't have to chase him all over town — which would be a reversal of what I understand is the standard situation; usually it's Spencer who's in swift pursuit of some female.

The sooner we meet, the sooner I can get to work. It would be great if he'd agree to get together this weekend, but that's probably an unrealistic hope. I have the incentive, my job is on the line, but Spencer doesn't know how urgent this is — and I'd like to keep it that way for two reasons. First, I don't want him to panic. Second, if he knows how badly I need these changes, it will give him the upper hand in any negotiating I might have to do. So I'll aim for a meeting on Monday, and if I can set one up earlier, that will be a bonus.

The plan, I decide, is to work at home tomorrow, which will give me tomorrow, Saturday, and Sunday to concentrate solely on Spencer's manuscript. Then, next week, with luck, Spencer's cooperation and twelve hours' work a day, I should make significant inroads on the novel and have something to show Hill on Wednesday.

I'd better stock up for the duration. I'll hit the supermarket tonight, wash the day's dishes, get a load in the washing machine, get to bed by 10:00 and I'll be ready to hit the decks at 6:00 tomorrow morning with a clear head and lots of energy.

# Chapter 6

I'M JUST ABOUT TO HEAD out the door — keys gripped resolutely in my hand, purse slung over my shoulder, the list of items I need to buy clear in my mind — when the phone rings. Groaning, I pause on the threshold. Do I rush back and answer it or sail blithely out the door, let fate take its course and the answering machine take the call?

It might be Jim. Maybe Em needs something I can drop off on my way to the store. I turn and dash up the stairs to intercept the machine.

"Hello?"

"Elaine Salter?" I vaguely recognize that voice, the raspy tone, the undercurrent of edginess. "This is Spencer Stone." After a moment's silence on my part, he adds, "Returning your call."

"Oh." My shopping list has flown out of my head; so has what I wanted to say to Spencer. Blankness yawns; the silence on my end of the line lengthens.

"Ms. Salter?" he says somewhat more sharply.

I remember now — I wanted to tell him what a disaster his novel is. Well, not that exactly. How do I put this diplomatically? "Sorry, I was just in the middle of something," I tell him. *Like my life, such as it is.* "I was hoping you'd be able to meet with me about *Sound and Silence.*"

"Before Monday? You were planning to call me Monday."

"Sooner, if possible." *Try to sound a little less eager, Elaine.*

"Why? Is something wrong?" His voice has grown sharp.

"Wrong?" I rush to reassure him. "Oh, no. What I've read so

far is fine." *Only fine?* I sense him thinking. "Very strongly written, intriguing," I amend, upping the flattery quotient. "I just want to go over a few minor points."

"Minor points," he repeats, sounding somewhat calmer.

"*Very* minor," I emphasize. "And it can't hurt to meet." I rush on before he has the chance to interrupt and ask why, if the points are so minor, the meeting can't wait until Monday. "The better I know you, the better I can do my job as an editor." I'm aiming here for a delicate balance: ingratiating, but sincere. I want to get my way without seeming to; I want to bend Spencer to my will without his realizing what's going on.

"Well, I don't know," Spencer says, but I can tell he's warming up to the idea. "I'm very, very busy."

Ah, playing hard to get, is he? *I don't doubt you're busy, what with all that extracurricular activity,* says the voice in my head. I tell the voice in my head to shut up — carrying on one conversation is hard enough without having editorial comments intrude.

"I understand completely," I say. "But I think it's very important for us to get together. This is the first time I've worked with you, and I want to be sure you're going to be comfortable with any editorial suggestions I might make."

"I see." He sounds interested. "Well. My secretary's gone for the day. I'll check my schedule with her tomorrow and see where I can fit you in."

*Fit me in? That's big of you,* my inner voice snaps. *I'll just put my life on hold until I hear from you, shall I?* "I'd appreciate it, Mr. Stone."

"I'll call you." The line clicks; he's gone.

*How did that exchange go?* I wonder as I turn the key in the ignition and my car sputters a couple of times. Spencer started off on the defensive, but I made soothing noises and calmed him down. I made a request that he didn't immediately accede to, but he probably will — *after* he's made it clear *he's* calling the shots. Right now he feels he's in charge, which is just fine, as long as I get what I want. All in all, I'd say it went moderately well.

Who knew publishing and love affairs had so much in common? Not me, when I first started in the business. And who knew so much seduction was involved? Writers, published and unpublished, desperately woo publishers; publishers pursue those writers who have a proven track record. Writers want to know they'll be respected in the morning; publishers want commitment, assurances that if sales go well, writers will stick around, justifying all the time, effort and money the publisher has expended on them.

Finally the motor turns over a couple of times. Right now Spencer and I are at the beginning of a relationship, I tell myself, easing up on the clutch and turning to negotiate my way backwards down the driveway. Whether it will be beautiful, or something entirely different, remains to be seen.

So I find myself, on the night before my thirty-fifth birthday, alone, pushing a shopping cart up and down the nearly empty aisles of a grocery store.

I love grocery stores. Something about them is reassuring: Maybe it's their clean shininess, their glistening chrome fixtures and dust-free shelves; maybe it's the helpful suggestions printed on glossy, recipe-sized cards posted here and there explaining how to serve the various products the store is selling — entertaining, and wildly optimistic about the amount of time the average person is willing to put into food preparation. Maybe it's the carefully organized abundance. People can't handle Nature's chaos of plenty — the seasons change and suddenly there are a million zucchinis to deal with; without warning the world is filling up with cherries — but in supermarkets the chaos is tamed and manageable, orchestrated in neat, tidy rows.

As I round the end of one aisle, a figure on the other side of the store catches my eye — Em. Something in the way she stands — the jaunty set of her shoulders, the confident tilt of her chin — tells me it's her. What is she doing here? She shouldn't be running around on her own. Where is Jim?

Just as I'm formulating the question, Jim steps into view, and in an instant I understand: he probably doesn't have any food at his house to make into a meal Em's willing to eat. When I first met him he seemed to subsist solely on yogurt, grapefruit, rice and copious amounts of coffee. I can imagine the conversation they had earlier:

"So, Em, what would you like for supper?"

"What is there?"

"Yogurt."

Silence.

"Rice?"

Silence.

"Grapefruit?" I hear resignation creeping into his voice as the realization dawns on him there's nothing here to make a meal of.

Silence.

"Well, let's go pick something up."

I back out of sight quickly before they can catch a glimpse of me, straight into a substantial woman who looks to be in her mid-fifties. She gives me a withering glance and "hmphs" in irritation as I take my foot off hers.

"Sorry," I mumble, scurrying away down the aisle to gather my thoughts in front of the phalanxes of cereal boxes mustered on the shelves.

One thing I have learned during my hours in grocery stores is you can tell what food fad is on the wane by wandering down the cereal aisle. For some reason, cereal manufacturers are about half a year behind any groundbreaking food developments. Six months after the hullabaloo about oat bran, I noticed a sudden proliferation of oat bran cereals: o's, flakes, with nuts and fruits (for the hedonists), without (for the purists). Two weeks later, when it was revealed oat bran was no better for you than any other kind of bran, it seemed to me the boxes of oat bran cereal exuded a certain existential *tristesse* — *sic transit cereal mundi.*

My impulse at this moment is to sail over and give Em a big hug, but then it would be difficult to tear myself away. Jim and I would strike up a conversation, and before I was aware of what I was doing, I'd be inviting them over for spaghetti dinner at my place, the evening would be shot, and I'd be no further ahead with Spencer's manuscript.

The lady I ran into is easing her way down the aisle, casting suspicious glances in my direction as she gets closer. I take a box of Korn Krunchies off the shelf and read the nutrition information on the side with intense interest.

But wait a minute — they're over in the cookie section. What are they doing there? Em doesn't need cookies, she needs good wholesome food. I'm going to have to talk to Jim about this.

"Hi, Elaine," he says as I swing into view. "Saw your car in the parking lot. Wondered when we'd bump into you."

"Hi, Mom. We're going to have a *gourmet* meal tonight," Em says, slipping beside me and wrapping her arm around my waist. I rest my arm along her shoulders. To an unsuspecting stranger, we'd look like a happy well-adjusted nuclear family discussing the relative merits of various cookies, instead of the bifurcated family unit we really are.

"Oh, really? Sounds nice."

"Lots of *vegetables,* Elaine," Jim says pointedly.

I glance at their grocery cart: lettuce, scallions, broccoli, red peppers — more vegetables, in fact, than I have in my cart.

"Would you like to join us?" Jim suggests playfully.

"No. I mean, yes, but I can't. I really have to sort out this novel."

"How's Hill the Pill?" Jim's pet name for my boss. Jim always had pet names for my bosses.

"Same as ever."

"Sweetness and light."

"I wish."

"Well," he rests his hand lightly on my shoulder. "Good luck. I'm sure you can pull it off."

"Good luck, Mom," Em echoes.

"Jim?"

He raises his eyebrows at me.

"I just remembered — my mother called. She's coming to town tomorrow and wants to take me and Em for dinner at the hotel at 5:30. I can pick her up —"

"Gram and Ed?" Em asks excitedly.

"Gram and Ed."

"Em and I are going to a craft fair in Tamworth tomorrow afternoon," Jim says. "I'll drop her off at your place by 5:00."

"Want to join us?" I add as an afterthought. Having Jim along would be useful, it would deflect attention from me.

"Absolutely not."

"Just an idea."

"Give me a call if your plans change. Emiloony here can stay with me as long as is necessary," he says, calling Em by her old nickname.

"I am not Emiloony." She giggles as I walk away.

"Are too."

Watching them leave, I feel an odd mixture of sadness and happiness. Em is such a great kid, and Jim's a wonderful dad. I'm sorry it didn't work out between him and me.

Although I know it would be crazy to give it another try, I miss him sometimes, his ability to keep things in perspective. And whatever other mistakes we've made, Jim and I have done a good job bringing up Em — she's full of energy, confidence and optimism. I sigh, feeling almost teary, as I push my cart toward the fast-food section.

I remember when she was a baby and we were a tight little family unit. To me it felt wonderful: comfortable, safe, perfect. The three of us fit together so well. It was very different from the family I'd grown up in. It wasn't until I was at university that I began to get some perspective on that family.

While the cart wheels squeak and the TV dinners tumble unbidden into my arms, a rush of déjà vu floods over me. Wandering around grocery stores was how I spent a good deal of time during my first year at university. Before Jim. Before Em. Before being sucked into the maelstrom of life. (Oh, that's a good one. Can I fit it into a press release for a book of poetry? That sort of exaggerated language works well with poetry. The limited number of words in poetry allows a lot of room for hyperbole in book blurbs and press releases.) Haven't I made *any* progress since then?

I was surprised to find myself at university; no one else in the family had ever attended one. Mother went to work cleaning houses when she was sixteen, and my father graduated from hanging around garages to selling used cars.

But Mother was determined I would get a university education. It had been an impossibility for her: my grandmother died when my mother was fourteen, leaving her in charge of four younger sisters and a brother. I was the focus of all her academic ambitions. "You have a good brain — you'll go to university." I wasn't going to argue; at that point university looked like the only way out of the house.

And I needed to get out of the house. It ran in the family. My father moved out when I was six after a series of spectacular arguments with my mother, which I still, as an adult, remember. It culminated with Mother changing the locks one day while Father was at work. When he came home, he couldn't get into the apartment. While they yelled at each other through the front door, Mother managed, with the assistance of our upstairs neighbour who thought Father was a lout, to get Father's car towed away from a no-parking area at the front of the building.

Father exits stage right; twelve years pass; adolescence rolls around. Mother and I found ourselves in the trenches. Not engaged in hand-to-hand combat, but whenever she picked up a knife, I left the kitchen.

The idea of university held a certain appeal, though not for the reasons Mother hoped. But it wasn't until I got to the university, was physically on campus amid the modernistic buildings that dotted the gently rolling, immaculately groomed lawns that the question occurred to me: Now what?

And all the space — physical (my own small apartment, uninvaded by Mother, inviolate) and intellectual — induced such a pitch of anxiety in me that I was paralyzed. I broke out in mysterious rashes on my face and arms; I couldn't sleep at night; I chewed my nails to the quick. Mother had counted on higher education opening the world to me; I'd be exposed to "influences," my horizons would be "broadened." She hadn't counted on agoraphobia.

It got to the point, finally, where I spent a couple of days in my apartment, in bed, curled on my side under my grey wool blanket. ("Grey's good," Mother had said when she selected it in the store. "It won't show the dirt.") As I lay there, with the weight of overdue essays and papers piling up on me and bearing down, I couldn't imagine how to get out of bed, let alone how to start ploughing my way through the backlog of work.

Eventually hunger drove me to the supermarket. Emerging

from my cocoon, I saw it as if for the first time. The lights, bright but not harsh, welcomed me. From the bakery the aromas of cinnamon, butter, and sugar drifted toward me. I had grown up in a house where potato chips, Cheez Whiz and soda pop were morally suspect. Marshmallows, Fudgee-os, TV dinners, frozen pastries, potato chips — I bought them all. I felt like my life — my *own* life — was finally beginning.

After that I gave up on classes entirely. Each morning I'd get up, fix an exciting breakfast — Pop Tarts, Eggo waffles, or Corn Pops, maybe — and settle down at the kitchen table with a book. That year I read Dickens, Eliot, Butler, Trollope, the Brontës, Austen — all fine solid books to start a day with, replete with characters, good and bad, and sturdy plot lines, nothing too unstructured or experimental that might unsettle my shaky sense of reality — and ate my way through every food innovation I could find. Once or twice a week, when supplies were dwindling, I'd venture out to the grocery store and the library.

Now here I am, in a supermarket once again. Our family unit — Em, Jim and me — isn't as seamless as it once was, but it's still pretty tight. Jim and I have managed to avoid most of the anger and acrimony that marked the end of my parents' marriage. For the longest time I hoped Jim and I could work things out, but our inability to do so doesn't feel like a failure to me now; instead it seems like a realization of our respective limitations. In the process, I've learned a lot about myself. Some of it I might rather not have known — my quite remarkable capacity for jealousy, for example. But there are other things I'm glad to have learned — for instance that a sense of humour can carry you beyond anger to something approaching tolerance.

I stop my grocery cart in front of an in-store display. Potato chips? No — cake is what I want. A chocolate log, big enough to accommodate thirty-five candles. On my way to the frozen desserts, I find a candle holder that plays "Happy Birthday" when the candle's lit. Perfect.

I picture setting the cake out on a plate, sticking it with so many candles that it bristles like a porcupine, then lighting the candles, making a wish and blowing them out. I imagine a knife slicing smoothly through the log and a rich, moist dark brown circle of chocolate cake tipping onto a plate. The thought of eating cake by myself depresses me. If Em were home, we'd make a party out of it: put on silly hats, eat the cake, make some popcorn and watch a video.

I decide I'll phone Kayla later and invite her over Saturday to celebrate. By then I'll have earned a break. She'll probably show up with a goofy joke gift, something that tweaked her sense of humour. Last year she gave me a clock powered by a potato. It still keeps pretty good time. I load up the bags and head home through the gathering dark.

# Chapter 7

At four in the morning I sit straight up in bed, suddenly awake, staring into the darkness. Counting sheep, folding imaginary laundry, running through the plot of Spencer's novel — nothing bores me back to sleep.

Forget F. Scott Fitzgerald, for me it's always 4:00 a.m. in the dark night of the soul. When Jim and I were first living together and money was tight, for weeks I'd wake up every night and stare into the glowering red LED display on the clock radio and wonder how we were going to pay the bills. "Four o'clock" the clock would glare until it glared "4:01." And even the boredom of this narrative didn't bring on drowsiness. Sometimes dawn would start to bleach the sky and I'd still be lying there awake, eyes fixed on the clock.

I could get up now and rattle around the empty house, but I figure I'll lie here and get some quality worrying done, get it out of my system. The possibilities for worry are so multifarious. There are the old regulars: money (lack of), health (failing, or is it just my imagination?), spontaneous human combustion (where did I pick this one up? I don't know, but it has figured prominently for years). There are the relatively new and unexplored areas of worry: retirement (when I'm eighty, if I'm lucky), strange noises in the car, terrorism. There's the BIG one: Em, which is comprised of many subsets: education, sex (when to tell her all, *or* what if she already knows it all, she's only ten for Chrissake), teeth, terrorism. And then there are the immediate sources of anxiety: job security (Spencer's novel), Spencer's novel (job security).

What I want to know is: What am I doing here? How did I end up in charge of *my* life, let alone my daughter's?

*If you'd only listened to me,* my mother's refrain, *and stayed in school; married a doctor/lawyer/professor, even; learned how to accessorize, how to economize, how to cook a decent pot roast — you wouldn't be where you are today.*

This is the same woman who once suggested, "Have you ever considered plastic surgery? I'm not saying your nose is big, but these little operations don't hurt much, and you'd be surprised the enormous difference such a small change can make professionally."

The woman who advised me cryptically, "Stay away from open-toed sandals. You don't want to attract attention to your toes."

"Why not?" I asked — this would have been when I was about twelve and wondering what open-toed sandals had to do with *any*thing.

"Just keep it in mind" was her response. "You have very nice hands."

My mother, who pointed out, "Don't get fat, dear. No one will want to marry you."

"Do you think I'm fat?" I asked, examining myself in the window of a store we were passing. I was about fourteen years old and hadn't yet made the jump to the adolescent section of the clothing store, I was still so small.

"Not yet," was her comforting reply.

By dint of sheer will and unwavering persistence, my mother has transformed herself from high-school dropout into the head of a small interior design company. "The Group," she calls it, which sounds slightly sinister to me. She attends seminars, reads trade magazines and is endlessly tinkering with how she presents herself to the world. Self-acceptance is not part of her lexicon; in her view, there's always room for improvement. She doesn't understand me, her feckless daughter who resists her good advice and seems to her to be completely content to wallow in a plain old untransformed self.

Where would I be now if my mother had had her way? In a house — my own, not a rental — a big one, a monster, three or four thousand square feet, with broadloom, and a Jacuzzi and central vac, although I wouldn't know about that in my mother's dream world because I'd have a "woman" come in to clean. You can break a fingernail vacuuming.

The house would be in suburbia, on a big lot, with a manicured lawn and scrawny little trees that flip over at the top and grow toward the ground looking like umbrellas.

In the best of all possible worlds, if I were the best of all possible daughters, I'd live up the street from her and Ed, her current husband. Ed's a laconic, easygoing man with a now-you-see-it-now-you-don't quietly ironic sense of humour. I get along better with him than I do with my biological father, who has the personality of a lamprey eel — he latches on and won't let go, and the longer he's around, the more he irritates.

At my wedding my father tried to sell Jim a used car. It was the first time I'd seen the man in three years, and he was giving my groom the gears. "It's a dream," he says. "Five years old and runs like new. Only 5,000 miles on it."

"We don't need a car, Dad," I told him. "I already have one."

"Listen, for you on your wedding day, I'll throw in free rust-proofing."

"No, Dad."

"Okay — *and* a free lube job."

I was ready to deck him. Jim merely looked puzzled. He didn't know a catalytic converter from a carburetor. My father might as well have been speaking Albanian for all the sense it made to Jim.

Finally Mother got Ed to lure Dad away with questions about the relative merits of second-hand Hondas compared to second-hand Valiants. This was generous of her, since she would have been happy if the wedding had been cancelled. She was disappointed with the son-in-law I'd selected for her. She'd been dreaming of saying "my son-in-law the doctor" or "lawyer" — even "professor" would have made her happier than "philosopher." When I told her Jim and I were getting married, her response was, "Why?"

"Because I love him."

"So? Love doesn't pay the bills. If you really love him, tell him to get a real job. The world doesn't need another philosopher. You know," she continued, "this isn't what I had in mind when I paid good money for you to go to university."

"No?" I said in mock surprise.

"Don't give me that, young lady," she snapped. "You should get a career. You think I like selling slipcovers to the blue-rinse crowd?" Most of her clients were elderly women whose tastes ran to Queen Anne furniture and pastel colours. This was frustrating for my mother, who preferred Danish modern and bright primary colours. "And none of this nurse or teacher nonsense," she continued. "You'll get enough of looking after other people when you're married and have a family." A business degree was what she had in mind, or something to do with economics. "You know what they say about money," she nodded sagely. "It makes the world go round."

"That's love," I corrected her.

She shrugged.

In my mother's dream world, I'd be the well-dressed, professionally employed, gracious helpmate of my husband, the doctor/lawyer/whatever. I'd make a nice home for him and the kids, wear nailpolish and have my hair done weekly. I'd entertain my husband's colleagues and their wives, meeting them at the front door of our impressive house and ushering them into the living room ("Yes, the cathedral ceiling really does make the room feel more spacious, doesn't it?") for a few cocktails before dinner, a gourmet meal catered by whoever's *de rigueur* these days.

This scenario makes my blood run cold. I am exploring the implications of it as I drift into a fitful sleep. I dream plates of complex hors d'oeuvres borne by disembodied hands floating through a shadowy, crowded room. There is a great crush of people I don't recognize. I circulate through the crowd, smiling, nodding and murmuring hello. I feel like an adolescent in a room full of grown-ups, and I have the sense everyone is staring at me with the quizzical condescension the adult world reserves for those who have stumbled outside the bounds of propriety, have burped or farted loudly in public.

Suddenly the doorbell begins to ring. I turn and try to make my way to the door, elbowing my way through the crowd, but there are too many people and my progress is slow. The doorbell continues to ring, droningly and insistently it rings and rings and rings —

*The phone.* I leap out of bed, nicking my foot on the corner of my chest of drawers in the process, run up the stairs and grab the receiver before the answering machine kicks in. *Ow ow ow.*

"Mom?"

"Em."

"You okay?"

"Yeah. I just whacked my foot." What time is it? Squint at the microwave oven across the room: 7:17. So much for rising with the sun.

"Dad said to call you so you know I'm up and off to school and won't have a hissy fit."

His exact words, no doubt. "How kind of him."

"He also said to tell you happy birthday."

"Thanks, sweetie."

"Do you want to talk to him?"

"No, that's all right. Don't forget to eat your veg and brush your teeth —" she groans audibly — "and I'll give you a call later."

"Okay, Mom."

"Not too much TV."

"Mo-om."

"Well, it was worth a try."

"Bye, Mom." And she's gone.

Great, I've barely started work on the book and already I'm behind schedule. Could this be a bad omen? Face it, Elaine, the whole book's a bad omen.

A cup of coffee, a Pop Tart, and a quick call to the office. I leave a message on the voice mail. "Jerri, it's Elaine. Could you please let Hill know I'll be working from home today? Just forward any calls."

I boot up my computer and get ready to shoot an e-mail off to my friend Paige. I'm going to take Kayla's advice and see whether Paige has any ideas about what to do in this situation and any info on Spencer. I dig my daily organizer out of my purse and flip to the "T" section of my address book. There's Paige's entry — look at all those crossings-out, that string of addresses adopted and abandoned, apartments rented and vacated, sublets, leases. I think back to Paige's first address, a modest bachelorette on the third floor of a brick house in the east end of Toronto. It stuck in my mind because her neighbourhood was so quiet and well heeled in contrast to the noisy, bustling part of the city where Jim and I lived.

I met Paige when Em was two, eight years ago. It seems so long ago, several personalities ago at least. In our salad days, which fell roughly after our rum-and-coke days and before our current high-fibre days. That time is a blur now. I was in the grip of Baby Brain; getting up every hour or two with Em had turned my brain to mush.

But I was happy then and the sources of my happiness were simple: Em and Jim. Em was, to my eyes, beautiful and endlessly fascinating. Jim seemed satisfied; there were no hints of discontent. My work was uncomplicated but interesting. I brought no worries home from the office. My world was small, but it contained everything I needed.

Paige was one of the reasons Jim and I decided to move to Kingston. She preceded us here; this is where she studied law. When Jim was looking at graduate schools, he was considering Queen's, and we asked her what it was like here. She said she liked it, although she's such a workaholic she's never yet managed to break free of her job at *City* magazine — the publication that brought her and me together — long enough to visit us here. And I seriously doubt that she ever took advantage of the coffee shops, bookstores and revue houses that make this place civilized even while she did live here.

Our paths first crossed back in Toronto soon after I got a job at *City*. The magazine had been born fifteen years earlier as *Street Life,* a small, sassy, street-smart tabloid. When success went to its head and swelled its bank account, the magazine reinvented itself as *City,* bigger, glitzier, more upscale — but still housed in the original rabbit warren of offices on the second floor of a warehouse.

When I was hired there, chunky manual typewriters had already been replaced by the smooth, ergonomic lines of PCs. The magazine was by then a four-colour affair printed on shiny coated paper instead of a tabloid run off on newsprint, but somehow the fact that we worked in offices where you risked concussing a co-worker if you stretched at your desk meant we were still keeping faith with the magazine's original renegade spirit. This was the theory, unspoken but implicit; in practice what it meant was there was no room for anyone or anything.

As the newest employee I'd been allocated a desk in a spare space in the front hallway. Though I'd been promised a cubicle of my very own as soon as some rearrangement of personnel freed up space, I'd spent almost a year sitting in the middle of a drafty hallway. Situated at the top of the stairs, I was the first person anyone encountered when they entered the office, and I was getting accustomed to signing for deliveries, chatting with bicycle couriers, and giving directions to the various offices.

Paige almost slipped by me unnoticed that first day. Her pale blonde hair, cut in a plain bob, hung to her shoulders. She wore a pale blouse and skirt so nearly the same tone as her hair that from a few feet away the details of her appearance blurred and she registered as a field of beige. "Excuse me," a low voice asked, "can you tell me where Editorial is?"

"Down there." I waved vaguely to the left. When the chaos of desks, chairs, people, and bicycles registered, I offered to take her there. As we made our way through the paraphernalia of magazine publishing — stacks of back issues, piles of subscription cards — I introduced myself.

"I'm Elaine Salter."

"Paige Turner."

To my addled, sleep-deprived brain — Em at two was still only sleeping for two-hour stretches — her name seemed unremarkable. Only later did it sink in. Page turner. Working in Editorial.

We pressed on through the clutter until we arrived at a large oak desk barring entrance to a large oak door. Paige had an appointment with the publisher himself, a reclusive type; it turned out she'd been hired as a summer intern. The following Monday, when I entered the meeting room for our weekly pep talk, there she was, sitting to the right of the managing editor. She wore a light grey suit, nearly the same colour as the walls of the room. The managing editor wanted to know why the magazine seemed to be losing female readers in the twenty-five to thirty-five year old age bracket. As the sole representative of working mothers in the room, I was quizzed on the reason for this circulation problem. My explanation that the only reading I'd done lately was on Tempra bottles at 2:00 a.m. by the glare of a night light was met by a murmur of laughter and blank incomprehension.

After the meeting broke up and everyone hurried off to their respective offices, I proposed to Paige that we do a little market research on the reading habits of working women in the twenty-five to thirty-five year old age bracket at my favourite coffee shop. The Maple Leaf was a crowded old greasy spoon where the regulars had been ordering the same food for so long that the owner, who was one of the two waitresses, usually had their plate on the counter in front of them before they'd finished ordering.

"Hi, George," she'd call as a wizened elderly man with a dusting of white stubble on his chin shuffled through the front door.

"Bacon and eggs —" he'd start.

"— with toast, hold the home fries, eggs over easy," she'd finish. "Here's your coffee," setting the mug down on the table in front of him.

In a booth at the back, over bacon and eggs for me, black coffee for Paige, Paige explained how she'd ended up at *City*. She'd originally wanted to do development work in the Third World — help people improve their lives, that sort of thing. A law degree was supposedly the way to go, so she got her degree at Queen's. But she'd found that the development community was a closed shop. One of her professors suggested *City*, and knew the publisher. That's how the internship had come about.

That was eight years ago. And the rest, as they say, is history.

We worked at *City* together for about ten months. I left; she stayed. And flourished. Today, Paige is one of the few staff members to have survived since my tenure at the magazine. The lives of those who work on magazines are often nasty, brutish, and short. The axe fell so frequently at *City* I would have felt right at home in a logging camp. Politically astute, intellectually brilliant, and somewhat addicted to work, Paige made her way from summer intern to book editor at one of the country's most widely read and influential magazines. She has cemented her position through a series of Machiavellian machinations and no one seems to be able to rout her.

Do I want to be Paige, swanning around to literary festivals in the company of internationally-recognized authors, having my opinion sought out on the current state of literature?

When Jim and I were coming apart, the answer would have been an emphatic yes. I dreamed of packing up and heading back to the city in pursuit of an exciting job like Paige's. It would have been fun, I thought, to rub shoulders with the movers and shakers. But parse that concept and you end up with a bad case of friction burn, cozying up to all those people jiggling around. By which I mean that it became clear to me, as my unhappiness subsided, that the hustle and bustle of city life wasn't for me. I like the pace of life here, and my present job, though currently crazy-making, is the best one I've ever had. Kingston is Em's home — her friends and school are here — and if I'm going to ask her to leave, I'd better have a good reason, not merely a vague sense of dissatisfaction. On top of which, Jim would have a fit if I decided to move away and take Em with me.

So here I stay, which means a solution must be found to this current situation — and Paige may help me find it.

"Hi, Paige." My fingers rush across the keyboard, outlining my predicament in the most cursory terms:

> Hope all is well. I need some advice. Hill just handed me a real challenge — Spencer Stone's novel, which has been in hiding for years, and, having read it, I know why. I've got one week to turn it into something publishable. If I don't, I'm out of a job — either Hill turfs me, or, if the book doesn't sell, Hunter is down the tubes. The novel needs a major make-over AND I've got to get Spencer onside to do it. Any ideas/info/pressure points you can suggest?
>
> Ciao,
> Elaine

Then I pop the message off into the Internet ether, and turn my attention to *Sound and Silence.*

Spencer's protagonist is presented as a deeply sensitive man locked in a thankless job and a loveless marriage, neither of which fulfils him. At least I think that's what Spencer's trying for. In fact, our hero comes across as self-absorbed and completely unempathic, given to long, ponderous internal discourses on the purpose of life — *his* life. If other people have lives, they don't make much of an impression on this guy.

Paralyzed by his situation, this fellow discovers that even his creativity, which has sustained him until now, is drying up. In an attempt to counter this inanition, he engages in several sexual encounters (all fairly explicit, most of them disappointing due to the callowness of the women involved), which throw into relief our hero's sagacity, tolerance and deep humanity, and confirms his sense that romance is dead. *Not that his behaviour is likely to revive it,* a little voice in my head mutters.

My guess is, this book will appeal to middle-aged academic types who'd like to do some similar engaging themselves but don't have the guts. Since these are the people who often write book reviews, this will work in our favour. But since the book-buying public is largely women, a little of the clinical detail will have to be toned down. And how much of the following can *anyone* stomach:

> She turned to him, her eyes wide pools of blue. He could fall into her eyes, eyes the colour of clear water on a cool afternoon in early spring, and wash away his pain, his desolation. "You understand," he said, and her smile was his answer.
>
> He gathered her into his arms, feeling her strength, feeling at long last his own answering strength. His face was lost in her hair. He drank in her smells, lost himself in all she was.
>
> He entered her and began, slowly, rhythmically, to move into her, deeper and deeper, his body hard against hers. And then they were sighing, murmuring to each other, her voice soft and faint at first, then growing stronger, more insistent. Further and further he took her, both of them riding the crescendo of sensation to its most distant limits.

Uh-huh. This kind of writing is enough to make me consider celibacy. With all that "further and further" and "distant limits," the passage reads like a squib about the space program, not a description of lovemaking.

And I've got to do something about the wife. There's long-suffering, and then there's masochistic, and the latter is definitely outdated in these post-*Backlash* days.

The painful truth is, not much happens in the novel. Over the course of a twenty or thirty page short story, this wouldn't be a problem; the stasis would serve as a metaphor for modern man's spiritual paralysis, emotional hollowness (apologies to Eliot), the futility of contemporary life or its moral decay — all the material that first-year university courses cover. But over the course of a three hundred plus page book, well, *oatmeal* doesn't begin to describe it. Maybe I should sacrifice a small animal to the god of best-selling novels to improve the book's chances.

I've read the entire manuscript, I have a sense of it, have some notes — now what? I decide I'll work through the hard copy, marking changes as I go. Then, if Spencer ever calls back so I can nail down a meeting time with him, I'll ask him to sit down with me and go through the edits I'll be suggesting. After that, I'll key in the changes he agrees to and print out the revised version. As long as he doesn't decide to rewrite the rewrite, I'll have a fairly clean copy of the manuscript at the end of the process to hand Hill Wednesday as planned. I pick up my pencil and tackle the first paragraph.

After a while I check the clock: 8:30. First I try Morris's number. It rings and rings, but no one picks up. His answering machine must be broken. Then I call Kayla. Just as I'm sure her answering machine's about to kick in, she picks up the phone.

"Hello?"

"Sleeping late?"

"Elaine — you know me better than that. I was in the middle of my yoga video. How are you?"

"Stressed. This book is a nightmare. I've been trying to get hold of Morris, but no answer. And I'm trying to pin Spencer down for an earlier meeting. On a completely different subject, can you come over and eat cake tomorrow?" I ask.

"In honour of what?"

"Today is my birthday, but I'm having dinner with my mother tonight."

"With bells on. What time tomorrow?"

"Sevenish."

"Isn't that kind of late for you? Don't you and Em usually eat around 6:00?"

"Em's staying with Jim for the duration."

"Why don't I take you out for a drink?"

"No, I can't. I've got to get through this book. But I'll need a break by then."

"Okay, rain cheque on the drink. See you tomorrow."

I settle back to work, and half an hour later, as I hesitate, considering whether to cut the second "moist" in as many sentences, the phone rings. To answer or not to answer, that is the question. It could be Hill or Em, it might be Kayla, it might even — hope makes my heart beat faster — be Spencer. "Yes?"

"Hello." A diffident voice, reserved.

"Nathan."

"Yes." He seems surprised I recognize his voice. "I spoke with the babysitter," he says, "and I wondered if you'd be free Saturday. She's busy every night until next weekend."

"Tomorrow?" Are those butterflies in my stomach?

"Unless you'd rather not," he says.

"No, I'd love to. I just — it's this book — how would you feel about coming over here?"

"That would be fine."

"What time's good for you?"

"Six, 6:30, if that's not too early."

"Sounds good."

Shall I cancel Kayla or not? No — I want them to meet. Later I'll pick her brain about him.

I let him know another friend will be here as well, and when I hang up the phone, I notice I've scribbled "NATHAN" several times in uppercase letters on the notepad I keep by the phone. Anxiety? Anticipation? Hard to tell. At any rate, if he's a serial killer, Kayla will discover my body before Em gets home and stumbles over it.

*Get a grip, Elaine.* He's just a normal guy. He'll show up and have a coffee. We'll sit and chat, both of us feeling a bit self-conscious and a bit foolish. I'll be wondering if he's noticed the wrinkles on my forehead and the chipped coffee mugs, and he'll be wondering if it's okay to smoke in my place and should he have brought something, maybe flowers, but he doesn't think that's appropriate yet, possibly later, if we start seeing each other on a regular basis.

After an hour or so I'll say I have to get back to work. He'll say goodnight and play with the idea of getting together again, but he won't ask yet. He'll want to go home and think about it. Will his son Isaac like me? Will I like Isaac? Should Isaac and I meet, or wait a while and see how it goes? It's rough on a kid to have people walking in and out of his life the way you walk through a revolving door. If I get along with Isaac but Nathan and I don't hit it off, how does he explain it to his kid? Better to take it slowly.

And for me, there's Em to consider — reconstituted families: blessing or curse? Probably been done on some TV talk show. But as usual, I'm getting ahead of myself.

Just as I admonish myself to snap out of it and get back to work, the phone rings.

"Hi, Elaine?" Ah, the dulcet tones of our office manager.

"Hi, Jerri. How can I help you?"

"Do you have the mailing list for next month's cookbook launch?"

"Not off the top of my head, no."

"Is it on your computer?"

Visions of Jerri turning on my computer and doing God-knows-what to it race through my imagination. "Janine has it on her computer," I say. "Get her to give it to you."

"All right. And Elaine?"

"Yes?"

"Things are fine here. Just so you don't worry."

*Well, I wasn't planning to until you mentioned it.* "Thanks, Jerri. That's good to know." I hang up. Now, not only do I have Spencer's manuscript to worry about, but thoughts about what Jerri is up to will dance through my head as well.

Once more the phone shrills. Probably Nathan calling. He's thought it through more thoroughly, reconsidered and wants to cancel. I pick up and sigh a resigned, "Hi," to whoever's on the other end. Expecting Nathan, I am greeted instead by Spencer's low-pitched rumble.

"Ms. Salter."

"Mr. Stone."

"I can meet you today between 3:00 and 5:00."

That gives me two hours to work on him and half an hour to make it to the hotel for dinner with Mother. Cutting it a bit tight, but I can do it. "I'm glad to hear it."

"At Hunter Press?"

"Ah — no, I'm working from home today."

"Fine, I'll come there."

In light of his reputation for womanizing, this idea makes me vaguely uneasy, but I tell myself to relax. I'm his editor, not a romantic interest. It's not as if I've ever driven men wild with passion. I'll put on my librarian persona and keep the focus firmly on punctuation and narrative structure.

"Ms. Salter?" There's a sharp insistence to his voice.

"Fine," I say. I give him directions and after he hangs up I review the conversation. The important thing, I decide, is that I got what I wanted — a meeting with Spencer.

# Chapter 8

By 2:30 A KNOT OF ANXIETY is slowly but insistently tightening inside me. What if Spencer won't accept the changes I'm suggesting? Was arranging a meeting with him a good idea? I should just have rewritten the entire thing, pushed it through production without showing him the edits, intercepted the proofs and let him discover the changes after the fact. Right, and I'm the Queen of Sheba. Let's stick with reality here.

So back to question number one: what happens if Spencer's unhappy with my improvements? He's got a lot of influence with Hill — he could simply sail into Hill's office and refuse to work with me. I am contemplating the depths of Hill's displeasure were this to occur, when the doorbell rings.

I go downstairs and usher Spencer in. He looks a bit rumpled. He may be coming from a long day at the university; alternatively, a short tryst with the poet might result in this wrinkled look.

He pauses on the threshold, his eyes flicking quickly around, surveying the disorder with barely disguised distaste.

"Please come in." I wave him past me. "We'll be working upstairs." I point toward the staircase. He makes a quick beeline in that direction, carefully picking his way past the laundry, firewood, bikes and other assorted miscellany.

Once he's settled at the kitchen-cum-dining-room table with a cup of coffee, I pass him the first few pages with the changes I'm suggesting. "I've reworked the beginning slightly. You mentioned you weren't totally satisfied with it." The words come out in a rush. I'm taking the offensive, using his own words to justify what I'm doing. "A lot of the action leading up to that point can be filled in later, but if you start in the car wash, you've got the reader's attention and the story's got a lot of momentum."

I settle back, waiting for his response. I don't have to wait long. As I watch him read, a wave of pallor rushes over his face, bleaching away the colour.

"What is this?" he demands. "You've gutted it!"

"No, no. Not really," I protest. "Well, maybe a bit. But I'd rather you thought of it as trimmed. Tightened up."

*"Tightened up?"* he repeats loudly. "Where's Juliana? What have you done with her?"

"I cut her," I admit.

"What? You can't just jettison a character outright."

I'd like to jettison a whole lot more than that, I want to say. But instead I merely point out, "Well, she talked too much. And, you have to admit, she didn't really serve much purpose. In a couple of instances there's a big, dramatic scene, followed by pages of Juliana — and sometimes Sullivan, too — rehashing what just went on. The effect is deflating; it stops the story dead in its tracks. Juliana doesn't move things along. She functions more as a chorus than a character. You have to trust your readers and assume they can follow the story and don't need to be hit over the head by a character saying, 'Here's what just happened. Get it?'"

Spencer throws himself back in his chair, one arm thrown across the now-tumbled papers on the table in front of him, the other draped over the back of his chair. I sense an inner battle raging silently: outrage over what I've had the temerity to do mixed with relief that someone's taken a stab at fixing the book. He sits, eyes fixed on the floor, jaw working, hair tumbling as he tilts his head to one side. *How does he get his hair to do that?* I wonder. Highlight his profile just so? Does he practise in front of a mirror?

After a moment's silent contemplation, he says, "I guess I shouldn't be surprised." He looks up at me with a wan smile. "You're probably right. It's my own fault." He leans forward, elbows on the table, eyes intent. "It's just that I want to put everything in. Life in all its complexities and contradictions: the grit, the grief, the triumph of the human spirit. People — *real* people — warts and all." He shakes his head, his expression serious.

I sit in stunned astonishment, not quite ready to believe my ears. Did I hear correctly? Did he just say I might be right? I expected more of a fight. Observing his disconsolate expression, I feel a twinge of guilt. Maybe I've been a little too hard on him. He looks so ... defeated. I don't want him to be totally demoralized — he might just abandon the book altogether. Perhaps a few words of encouragement are in order. It's not as if the novel's badly written — at least, parts of it aren't. It just needs some modification.

"I think you've succeeded admirably," I tell him. "It's very ... inclusive. It's got — there's a lot of strong writing. The biggest changes I'm suggesting — and these are only suggestions — are at the beginning. As we continue working, you'll see a lot of the changes I'm looking at are fairly minor. Overall, I think the story just needs a little shaping."

"You think so?" He seems to perk up. "Just a little shaping?"

"Absolutely."

"If I grant you that some changes may be necessary," Spencer begins cautiously after a moment's silence, assessing me through narrowed, measuring eyes, "I want you to understand that doesn't mean I'm prepared to accept all of them — or even most of them. This is my book, my name on the cover."

"This is your book."

"And you're just attending to details."

Clarifying the ground rules, is he? As long as I get the changes I need, that's fine by me. "I'm just tidying up," I say in a placating tone.

"As long as we agree on that," he says.

An hour later I'm not so sure. I may have misjudged the competition. Clearly, my definition of "minor" doesn't correlate with Spencer's. In the time we've been working, we've managed to cover a total of two pages. I'll call it negotiating, although it's more like a little tussle in every instance. We *negotiate* nearly every letter on the page, it seems to me.

"No, no, no." Spencer shakes his head. "The comma has to stay. Don't you see how it changes the cadence there, shifts the emphasis onto *alone*? 'And then, he turned off the light and stood in the darkened room, alone,'" he reads reverently. "See how subtly it reveals his essential loneliness and isolation without saying outright he is lonely and isolated?"

I glance at my watch. We've spent five minutes on these twelve words. At three hundred words per double-spaced page, this equals about two hours per page, which translates roughly into fifty twelve-hour days for this book — if there are no interruptions.

"Fine," I say. "Leave the comma in. Now if we can move on to the next page —"

"Hold on." Spencer raises an admonitory hand. "If we leave in that comma, I think the one in the next sentence needs to stay, too, for balance."

At this rate, I decide, the book won't be finished until next season. But I won't be around for the book launch. I'll be dead — Hill will murder me.

Spencer keeps trying to reintroduce Juliana, but I continue to resist her reappearance. Why is he so determined to put her back in when she's completely ancillary to the story? Has he promised his current squeeze he'll give her a cameo in his novel? Is that why he's so insistent? We struggle with the question for several minutes — Spencer gaining ground for a few moments then falling back before my incisive arguments — before I finally claim victory.

Maybe it was a ploy, his speech about grief and stuff. Maybe he was defusing me, pushing my sympathy buttons, making me feel sorry for poor, beleaguered Spencer who just wants to bring grit and lint into readers' lives.

Spencer is preparing to argue with me about the use of "toward" versus "towards," when I spring to my feet. "More coffee?" I offer, determined to put distance between us lest I grab my pencil and start jabbing at the parts of him within range.

"Yes, thanks," he replies evenly, evidently oblivious to my irritation.

While I'm bustling around, Spencer says, "I think we've made good progress. It's as Flaubert observed, 'I spent the morning putting in a comma, and the afternoon taking it out.'" He grins self-mockingly to show he's not seriously putting himself in the same league as the author of *Madame Bovary*, although I suspect Spencer really does think his talent is comparable.

Even though I grin back for civility's sake, I, however, staring possible unemployment in the face, am not amused. *Buddy,* I'm thinking, *you're not Flaubert.* If you were, this would be a much better book, and I would be looking forward to *Sullivan's* suicide. Which is an ending I could live with. But I recall a conversation I had with Em. "Sometimes when you get going on a rant," she told me, "and I can't get you to stop, all I can do is smile and nod, smile and nod until you're finished." That seems to be the best tactic with Spencer now: smile and nod.

We continue working from word to word, line to line, which is not what I want to be doing right now. Now is the time for a general edit. We should be working on the novel's overall structure, on tightening chronology and pacing. The line edit comes later.

At times my patience wears thin. There's a point when I'm tempted to ignore my earlier reservations and snap, "Fine, we'll publish it the way you wrote it, if that's what you want." The words are on the tip of my tongue when Spencer notes, in reference to a passage involving several flashbacks that had required some temporal fine-tuning, "I think you handled this very well. It's much clearer now."

After that, the pace picks up and we make steady if not remarkable progress. By small — very small — increments my anxiety diminishes, although it doesn't entirely abate. The little flares of snarkiness I sensed were informing some of his remarks earlier appear to die down. I begin to feel he may be coming around to seeing things my way.

And I begin to understand why some women might respond positively to Spencer. His manners are courteous to an almost exaggerated degree. "Thank you very much," he says when I set the carafe of coffee on the table in front of him. "That's very kind of you."

Not so kind really, since I'm in dire need of caffeine myself, but I'll take positive feedback where I can get it. "You're welcome," I reply. I might as well make use of all the etiquette Mother drilled into me.

He's playful, in an awkward, heavy-footed way, and despite a tendency to take himself very seriously, there are flashes of humour

— as in the Flaubert comment. I'm not convinced he's as humble as all his self-deprecating asides would suggest. I sense a core of undiluted pride, but he does listen to what I have to say, even if only to disagree with it. Some other men are altogether deaf to the sound of a woman's voice. So, although he's not making this easy, he doesn't present as the complete jerk I'd been led to believe he would be.

By the end of the afternoon, Spencer's spirits have risen visibly. He's much more relaxed, and the undercurrent of hostility I sensed earlier has dissipated. "We make a pretty good team, wouldn't you say?" he asks, flashing me a grin.

"Things seem to be going well," I allow, tapping the marked-up pages in front of me into a tidy pile.

He checks his watch. "A quarter to five," he says. "I didn't realize it was so late. I really must go." He stands, shrugs on his jacket. "There's still a lot of ground to cover," he says. "We need to meet again tomorrow."

"I think that's a good —"

"Ten," he continues. The word is less a question than a statement. He collects the pages on his side of the table and slips them into his briefcase.

"Ah, that's a bit —" *early,* I'm about to say, but Spencer continues as if my agreement is a given.

"See you tomorrow, bright and early. Don't get up," he says. "I know the way out." Before I have time to say anything, Spencer has headed down the stairs and I hear the door swing shut behind him.

While I am tidying the table, it occurs to me to wonder where Em is. Jim said he'd drop her off, and we have to be at the hotel to meet my mother in half an hour. A moment later the phone rings.

"Elaine, Jim."

"Where are you?"

"I'm on my way. Something burned out in the car — black smoke everywhere."

"How's Em?"

"We're both fine, thank you for asking," he says, an edge to his voice. "I'm at a garage in Harrowsmith, and the guy here says it's either oil on the engine or the heater core imploding. Either way,

I'm running late. But we're on our way. I'll drop Em off at the hotel."

"Right. See you there."

Twenty minutes later I'm waiting in the hotel lobby when Jim, looking definitely the worse for wear, and Em, looking as though she's had an excellent adventure, walk through the sliding doors. Em is delighted at the prospect of dinner at the hotel.

"This is the place where I get a little paper umbrella in my drink," she says excitedly.

"Be still my heart," Jim replies.

"The car blew up," Em says with undisguised elation. "Dad could barely see. It smelled gross." A faint scent of burned oil or other automotive material wafts in my direction.

"The mechanic said it's probably not the heater core since they almost never burn out," Jim says, sounding slightly less glum than he did over the phone.

"That's good. It costs a lot to replace a heater core."

We're standing in an environment composed almost entirely of glass, chrome and stainless steel, mirrors reflecting in mirrors. You can see yourself over and over again if you want. I don't.

Beside us Em stands, percolating with anticipation. After a moment she ducks away to prowl around on the suspicion Gram and Ed have taken another route down and will spring from behind one of the glass-lined pillars to surprise her. At one point she sets off down a corridor to investigate.

"Don't go too far," I call after her.

Jim and I are discussing the car when across from us the shining elevator doors sigh open and I watch a couple disembark.

*There's Ed,* I think, *but who's that little old lady with him and where's Mother?* A second later understanding dawns: *Oh.*

Suddenly Em is racing toward them, arms flung wide, calling, "Gram," and Mother is smiling and saying, "Well, Emily," in a pleased tone of voice.

I cross the floor, smiling, and lean over to hug Mother. The cords of skin under her chin that make a parallel track down the front of her neck have grown more pronounced since I last saw her.

When I wrap my arms around her, there is less of her to hold. It's as if her flesh has receded and her bones have risen to the surface. She is all angles and knobs and edges, as sharp almost as the shock of how suddenly she's become old.

"Hello, Elaine," Ed says, wrapping me in a bear hug. "How's the birthday girl?"

"I'm fine, thank you, Ed."

"Hi, Jim," Ed says, clapping Jim on the shoulder. "Long time no see."

"Hello, James," my mother says. "How are you?"

"I'm fine, Shirley."

"How's the house-painting business?"

"Just fine, thank you."

She casts an appraising eye over his faded jeans, white T-shirt and blue windbreaker. "You don't dress like you own a company," she says.

"That's because I *am* the company," Jim replies. To the un-initiated, he might sound calm; I, however, can hear the under-current of irritation creeping into his voice.

"Still, if you want to make a good impression on people, you need to dress the part. The more professional you look, the more confidence you inspire, the more business you'll get," she says.

I can see Jim's patience rapidly evaporating. "Ed," I say, "Jim had a little problem on the way here. Could you take a look at the car and see if you can figure out what it is?"

"Sure, I'll give him my two cents' worth," Ed says, and the two of them head toward the parking lot.

"I'll drop Em off later," I call after them. Jim nods vaguely, then turns to catch what Ed is saying.

"Happy birthday, Elaine," Mother says in a perfunctory way. I can understand her lack of enthusiasm. If I'm getting older, it means she is too.

"Thank you."

She turns her attention to Emily. "And how is my favourite granddaughter?"

"I'm your *only* granddaughter," laughs Em.

"How tall you're getting. How is school?"

"I got an A on my medieval castle project," Em says.

Mother nods approvingly as we make our way to the restaurant. A few minutes later, Ed joins us. "Probably the heater core," he says, shaking his head, as he takes a chair beside Mother. "Big ticket item."

"Well that's too bad," Mother says with absolutely no sympathy in her voice. "Now, Elaine, let's go have a nice meal in honour of your birthday, and you can tell me about this book you're working on."

The meal passes surprisingly smoothly. Memories of birthdays past give the occasion a piquant flavour. "Eat," she'd say, pressing plates of cake at my friends, already stuffed with candy. "Time for fun," she'd call like a crazed phys. ed. teacher, subjecting us to a series of tightly choreographed games — not a moment left to chance. As if, by the sheer force of her will, a good time would be had by all. I can recall the teeth-gritting atmosphere of those parties as clearly as if they happened yesterday.

In contrast, it's a relief to be here today, just her, Ed, Em and me sitting in the faux-French provincial decor of the hotel restaurant. I am a grown-up now; I can decide what I want to eat, and I'm under no pressure at all to pretend I'm having a good time.

But I enjoy myself. The food is good, the wine pleasant. Ed is a skillful raconteur who keeps Em in stitches, and Mother seems content to let him do most of the talking. I check my watch at one point and am surprised to find an hour has slipped away.

"We have to get moving soon, sweetie," I tell Em.

"Not before you've had some dessert," Mother protests.

"Please, Mom?" Em says.

"It is your birthday," Mother points out.

"Okay." I decide. "It's only once a year."

"I thought about ordering a cake and having everyone sing 'Happy Birthday,'" Mother tells me. "But I decided not to."

The idea of the wait staff approaching the table, cake in hand, singing the regulation birthday song makes me cringe.

Half an hour later Em and I rise to leave. "I know you're busy," Mother says to me, "but I don't get to see Emily nearly enough.

How about a movie tomorrow afternoon while Ed's at his reunion?"

"Aren't you going with him?" I ask.

"And talk to who? Engineers' wives? I'd be bored to death. How about a movie, Emily?"

"Sure." Emily is delighted at the prospect.

"You want to join us?" Mother addresses me.

"Mother, I told you — I don't have time."

"Can't hurt to ask."

"Thanks for a great meal," I say, grabbing Em's hand. "And thanks for not making everyone sing 'Happy Birthday.' I'll arrange things with Jim about tomorrow and give you a call." Before she has a chance to add anything, we're on our way out the door.

"See you tomorrow, Emily," I hear her call just before the doors whisper shut behind us.

I drop Em off at Jim's. "Mother wants to take her to a movie tomorrow afternoon. I said I'd talk to you and call her."

"Can you go brush your teeth, Emiloony? I'll be up in a minute to read you a story," Jim says. As soon as she's gone, he turns to me. "I don't want your mother coming over here," he tells me. "I'll meet them at the theatre. 'You don't dress like you own a company' — I haven't seen the woman in four years and she's going on about my clothes. I'm a house painter and the only reason I own the company is because there are no other employees."

"You know my mother. She's had a tough life," I say. "Pulled herself up by her bootstraps. She can't help it."

"That may be true, but she doesn't get to make my life tough, too. I don't know how you put up with it, Elaine," he says, shaking his head. "Never have."

"She's my mother. You don't get to pick your parents."

"Get back to me with the time, and I'll get Em to the theatre. Providing the car doesn't disintegrate further."

Back home I spend a couple of hours on Spencer's book and make a few more fruitless attempts to reach Morris before going to bed.

# Chapter 9

SATURDAY

I wake the next morning and discover there's no underwear in my dresser drawer. In the laundry room, I find clean laundry over-flowing from three baskets. Before Spencer invaded my life and metastasized into every corner of it, I was hoping to get these mountains of clothing folded over the weekend. That's not going to happen now. Wrinkliness is my fate for the foreseeable future. I'm reduced to digging around until I come across something suit-able. I'm working my way through a pile of towels and T-shirts when an image of Mother comes to mind. Not the mother of last night — short, perennially tan, firmly soignée, her now-blonde hair lacquered back off her face, trying for youthfulness but not quite succeeding — but the mother of twenty-five years ago: slight and dark, in constant motion.

The images come in pieces and fragments, less the narrative of history than snapshot glimpses of recollection. "I'm not your Mommy," she said to me once in a small bright kitchen with pale yellow walls, a Formica-topped table and, on the table, a jar con-taining a twig with a cocoon attached to it. Mother sat at the kitchen table folding laundry with quick, precise motions. I had found the twig while we were out for a walk, and Mother had agreed to let me bring it home and put it in a jar. She had told me a butterfly would come out of the cocoon soon, and I was waiting for the day the dull grey bundle would blossom.

The kitchen, the jar and the cocoon place the conversation in the apartment where we lived while my father still held full membership in the family. She must have said this to me around the time I was five or six.

"Only babies call their mother 'Mommy.' I'm your mother. Call me Mother." At the time her remark didn't seem unusual. What I vividly remember is the cocoon and how much I wanted to see the butterfly. Mother's statement was secondary. I remember the sentence in the context of the butterfly, not the butterfly in the context of the statement. Her words didn't surprise me, so I have to assume this wasn't the first time I'd heard them. They were familiar, part of the landscape, like the pale yellow walls.

Would I say this to Em? I can't imagine ever doing it. My impulse is always to draw her closer, shrink the space between us. When she was a baby, she was perfectly happy to let me carry her everywhere, but recently she's stretched out into string-beanness. She insists on her own autonomy and only now and then deigns to let me hug her. When she does, it's always on her terms.

Now I'm armpit-deep in laundry when I should be working on Spencer's manuscript. *Snap out of it,* I tell myself, *time's winged chariot is just around the bend. Get moving.*

I dress and make myself some toast then ascend to my roost, where I reread yesterday's work. My efforts seem to have had some effect; from deplorable, the manuscript has improved to nearly mediocre. But there's still so much to do — and Spencer's due here at 10:00.

First, another attempt to reach Morris. No luck. Then I hit the speed-dial button for Kayla's number. I'm nervous about dinner tonight; I need a shot of her confidence. I reach her answering machine. Her plummy professional tones fall into my ear full and round and rich as ripe cherries. I smile; she sounds so civilized, but I know the truth — I've seen her with half a bottle of Jack Daniels on board. At the beep: "Hello Kayla. Just calling about tonight."

I push the anxiety out of my head and apply myself to the manuscript for a while until a headache begins to grumble in my temples and it occurs to me I haven't had my customary three cups of coffee. The headache must signal the onset of caffeine deprivation.

While the coffee's brewing, the phone rings.

"Listen," Kayla says. "Tonight's fine. Quit worrying. And I think I may have some interesting gossip about Spencer. I was talking to the wife of a faculty member — I sold them the sweetest little place — and I get the sense —" I hear a click on the line. "Whoops. Incoming call. I'll see you tonight." And Kayla's gone, evaporated into the telephone void.

For an hour or so I concentrate on the pages in front of me, whittling away. I rejig a couple of scenes, breaking up a couple of long passages of reminiscence with some of the activity that's going on in the present, just to keep things moving. The book is gradually pulling together, and I'd feel a sense of relief if the question of Spencer's co-operation weren't always nagging at me like an irritating ad jingle looping on permanent rerun through my brain.

At 9:00 I phone Mother. "I think the matinee at 2:00 would be best," she says. "That way the pop and popcorn won't spoil her dinner."

I call Jim and pass along this information.

"Tell your mother I'll drop Em off at the theatre at a quarter to and pick her up there after the movie, will you?"

"Sure."

"And can you ask her to cut me some slack, Elaine?"

"I'll do my best. I haven't noticed that it helps."

Before getting back to work, I call Mother. "Mother," I say when I'm routed through to her. "Jim says he'll drop Em off at the theatre at a quarter to and pick her up there after the movie."

"Isn't that nice of him."

"Don't start, Mother," I say sharply. "Jim's a good father."

"Good fathers don't walk out on their children."

"That's between him and me. It doesn't involve Em. The two of them get along really well."

"Okay, okay, I'll keep my opinions to myself. You sure you don't want to join us?"

"I told you, I'm really busy," I hiss through gritted teeth.

"So get to work," she says, and hangs up. I override the impulse to throw the phone across the room, and return to the kitchen table.

I'm trying to untangle a rather involved sentence and a series of sexual manoeuvres I've never encountered in real life when my thoughts are interrupted by the ringing of the doorbell. Is it 10:00 already? I check my watch — yes, indeed, that must be Spencer at the door.

Today he's dressed more casually than he was yesterday, in a dark shirt and jeans. He's more cheerful, too.

"Good morning," he says when I open the door.

*It would be a lot better morning if Em and I were at the bakery now picking up cinnamon buns.* But, of course, I do not share this sentiment. I simply smile and wave him in.

Spencer passes me some of the material he took away yesterday. "I think I can work with many of your suggestions," he says. "Not all," he adds quickly. "And I've made some changes you'll need to look at."

I recognize this statement for what it is: he's staking out his territory — this is his novel, and he's going to make the final call. Fine by me, as long as *his* novel is in first proofs in two weeks.

Back at the kitchen table, we work through our respective piles of paper in relative quiet. As I read, I find that occasionally he's accepted my edit outright, indicating this with a small checkmark in the margin. More often, he's modified what I've proposed — frequently his justification is longer than the actual change he's proposing, his crabbed handwriting snaking up the side of the page and crowding the top margin. I note that despite such outbursts, by and large he's letting me rework the book; he's just fussing over details to maintain appearances. This is jim-dandy: he can have the commas, "toward" or "towards," "further" "farther" — his choice — as long as I control the plot structure, dialogue, characterization and thematic development.

"Elaine?" Spencer's voice breaks in on my thoughts, surprising me so that I jump.

"Sorry." He grins slightly. "I don't bite, you know. I just wanted to say, I hope I wasn't too brusque yesterday. You'll have to admit, some of the changes you suggested were rather drastic. And things are a bit chaotic at the university these days."

My automatic impulse is to be conciliatory, to say something vague and non-confrontational like, *Oh, that's okay.* This time, though, I stifle the impulse. "I'm sorry to hear it."

"Yes," he nods, frowning. Then he shakes away whatever thoughts are bothering him. "Anyway, this is sort of a trial by fire for you, isn't it?" He indicates the two stacks of paper. "Or are you accustomed to this kind of thing?"

"Oh, no. No, no." I shake my head emphatically, hoping to give the impression that scrambling at deadline in this undignified manner is an anomaly for those of us who work at Hunter Press; we are always completely on top of every situation, relaxed, competent, in control.

"How long have you worked at Hunter?"

I shrug. "Several years."

"Our paths never crossed before."

*You just weren't paying attention.* "Morris was Senior Editor," I reply.

"Do you like the job?"

"It's the best job I've ever had. Never a dull moment." I neglect to add I might enjoy a few more dull moments, a little less excitement. "I love books, I enjoy working with people —"

"Surely not neurotic writers?" he interjects, with a small smile that's meant to be self-mocking.

"They're not all neurotic." *Ninety-five percent of them are,* I'm thinking. *But that leaves — hey! — five percent who are sane, well-balanced individuals.* I wouldn't want to have to tell him into which group I would place him.

Spencer leans back in his chair. Light glances off his glasses, obscuring his eyes and the expression there. "How did Hill find you?"

*Find me?* An image flits through my mind of Hill picking up a rock and peering under it, frowning, then replacing it before moving on to the next one.

I shake off the feeling that Spencer's grilling me. "My husband" — I quite consciously omit the prefix "ex" — "decided to do his PhD at Queen's. We moved from Toronto. Life here has taken some getting used to."

He nods. "Yes, that's been my experience, too. It's like living in a fishbowl." I notice a certain sharpness to his tone. "You've done quite a bit of work on this." He lifts a piece of paper from the stack in front of him.

*Damn right.* "Hill wants to see first proofs in two weeks." I tell him. "Your novel's in the fall catalogue. If it doesn't get printed and into the stores in time, we'll miss the Christmas season."

"That would be too bad." Is there a subtle undercurrent beneath those words, the merest suggestion of a threat?

"Yes, it would. As I'm sure you know, if we miss Christmas, there won't be any point in releasing it until spring, and then we'd miss next Christmas' sales. Spring sales are okay, but the best time to hit the market is before Christmas."

Spencer smiles. "My concern, of course, is putting out the best work I can." The smile doesn't reach his eyes. "Sales are a secondary issue, as far as I'm concerned."

I stare at him for a moment. *What are you saying?* I'd like to ask. *That it doesn't matter to you if the book gets published? That you don't care how well it sells?*

"I don't want to publish anything less than the best book possible." I smile back. *Just as long as it's in the stores before Christmas,* I think.

"Good." His smile has evaporated. "I just want to make sure that we understand each other. I have to be completely confident about what goes into print," he says. "I wouldn't want Hill to have to be in the position of deciding who to back if there's a difference of opinion, you or me." Our eyes meet; Spencer's are cold.

In my mind's eye I measure the books I've worked on — the book of essays, a couple of volumes of poetry, *Highways and Byways* — against Spencer's books. I know, from having seen sales figures, which stack of books generates the most money for the press. It's clear where Hill's loyalties will lie.

"Now," his tone switches abruptly to businesslike before I can muster a reply, "about this passage you've cut here. I really think ..." and we're back into the thick of things. Once again Spencer is lobbying to reinstate the garrulous Juliana while I'm trying as diplomatically as possible to keep her out.

After a particularly intense episode in the trenches, I get up to refresh my coffee. Standing at the kitchen sink, I hear a sound behind me. The rumours jump to mind. My heart skips a beat — could it be Spencer sneaking up on me? I glance quickly over my shoulder, but no one's there. Spencer is at the table, hunched over a stack of paper. I take a deep breath, tell myself to relax and get back to work.

Finally, after another couple of hours, Spencer glances at his watch. "Is that the time?" he asks. "I really must be going." He stands, gathers up a portion of the revised manuscript we've been labouring over and slips it into his briefcase. "I'll keep working on it tonight. What time shall we meet tomorrow?"

"What's good for you?" He's coming back — a good sign, I'm telling myself, since I'm still not entirely clear about what passed between us earlier.

Face averted, he's fussing with the latch on his briefcase, his eyes avoiding mine. I sense the odd, slightly sinister push-pull that goes on when one of the parties in a relationship is pursuing a hidden agenda. What Em calls my spider senses — the way I can tell if she hasn't brushed her teeth or done her homework when she assures me she has — they're tingling now. The situation is so similar to what used to go on between Jim and me near the end of our time together that I'd laugh if I weren't on the verge of exploding with frustration.

"Ten," he says.

"Fine."

He picks up his briefcase. "It's nice to have this opportunity to get to know you. I look forward to spending more time together tomorrow. If it weren't for the fact that we're pulling my book apart, I might almost say this process is a real pleasure."

*What's his game?* I wonder, listening to his feet tap out a riff as he heads down the stairs. I don't want to badger him — I don't want to antagonize the man — but I'd like to know what's going on.

# Chapter 10

THINGS I'D LIKE TO DO RIGHT NOW: shake Spencer, pitch a fit, eat a box of cookies. Since none of these is an option — not a cookie in the house; I'd probably break part of myself or the house if I pitched a fit; Spencer's much bigger than I am, definitely not shaking material — I decide to have a brew and sit and stew. At least he's committed to coming back tomorrow. I'll take that as a good sign in the absence of any other good signs.

I carry my coffee into the living room, where I settle into my soft, overstuffed couch and turn my mind to comforting thoughts to take it off Spencer's anxiety-inducing behaviour. Em — suddenly I want to hear her voice — the need is a physical ache.

When she was little I carried her every moment I could. Her weight in my arms, her solid roundness, was the ballast that kept me level. Now, if she's not around for a long period of time, it's as if part of me is missing. I'm so accustomed to experiencing myself through contact with her — *these are my fingers tangled in her hair; these are my arms wrapped around her* — that when she's gone, I lose a sense of where I end and where the rest of the world begins. I start to feel wispy and insubstantial, like a photograph bleaching to invisibility with age.

The sound of the doorbell rouses me from these thoughts. Downstairs, I open the door to find Nathan. In front of him slouches a tow-headed boy who obviously wishes he were elsewhere.

"Isaac, this is Elaine Salter," says Nathan.

Isaac averts his eyes with the regal disdain of a proto-adolescent.

"Isaac." Nathan's voice is heavy with warning.

"Hi," Isaac mumbles in my general direction without looking at me. Apparently my rusting Tercel, parked further up the alley, is of more interest than I am. Behind him, Nathan shakes his head ruefully.

"We thought we'd drop by and see how it's going — whether tonight is still on, and whether you'd like to come out for a bit of fresh air," Nathan ventures.

"*You* wanted to, Dad," Isaac corrects him pointedly. In his remark I recognize the fierce resolution not to be pulled into duplicity that Em displays. *You old grown-up, get on with your lies, but don't sully me with them.*

I check my watch. Four o'clock already? "Oh, yes. I'm good for tonight. Getting a bit cabin crazy. And I have a question for you, so if it's all right with Isaac" — at the sound of his own name, Isaac's eyes slide toward me — "I'd like to come along for a few minutes."

Isaac gives the matter some thought. He's uncomfortable under the scrutiny of both adults but happy to have the power to grant or withhold permission. "Okay," he says finally. "If we can go to the park," referring to the grassy area at the top of the hill which was formerly a pioneer cemetery and now offers slides, swings, jungle gyms, a wading pool and a pile of rocks to climb on.

"Fine by me," I say.

I collect my jacket and keys. A moment later we're heading up the hill to the park. Isaac runs ahead.

"Wait at the corner," Nathan calls, slowing Isaac's trajectory slightly. "He's pretty careful, but sometimes he doesn't look," he tells me, then lapses into silence. After a moment he says, "I hope we're not disturbing you. You did mention you'd be working all weekend, and I thought you might like a break."

"No, it's fine. If I sit in one place too long, I ossify. And I really do have a question for you. You're a book person; have you read any of Spencer's work?"

Nathan nods.

"Do you think he's a good writer?"

Nathan considers the question as we catch up to Isaac and cross the street together. Once on the other side, Isaac breaks away and races off to the playground a block further along. "I think he writes quite well, but he may be out of his depth in a novel. The short story is the perfect scale for his talent. He's a miniaturist." Again I notice the careful precision of his speech.

"'Two inches of ivory.'"

Nathan replies wryly, "Spencer works on about a half inch of ivory. There's the question of character; most of Spencer's stories feature one or two characters, and novels need to be more densely populated than that.

"And then there's the question of form. A short story is sort of like a first date: it doesn't matter if you don't like the characters, because you're not going to spend much time with them. They just need to be interesting, or the situation does. A novel's more a matter of prolonged intimacy. It's hard to spend time with characters the author seems to feel contempt for. My guess is Spencer has trouble with intimacy."

A bit of veiled sniping in Spencer's direction, I note. I wonder what's bugging Nathan. Surely he's not jealous just because Spencer gets lucky with women?

We reach the perimeter of the park and stop. In sight of Isaac, who's in full flight on a swing, we stand silently.

"Well," I venture. What I feel like saying is: *What's going on here? Is this some new style of dating I don't know about? Could you please fill me in?* But though the minds and behaviour of the males of the species are no clearer to me now than they were twenty years ago when my hormones started running, I have learned from experience that direct questions often spook them. They'd rather talk about baseball. Since I haven't got a clue about baseball — or any other sport — I wrack my brain for something to say, only to draw a complete blank.

"Well." He's watching Isaac, frowning slightly. He sounds irritated, or maybe preoccupied.

"Is something wrong?" I ask.

"What?" He turns to me. "No, nothing."

He obviously means *Yes, something.* I want to tell him about what went on this morning while Spencer and I were working. I'd like to get his perspective on it. Maybe he could interpret what Spencer's up to. I want to find out what he knows about him, but something stops me. I get the feeling he doesn't want to discuss Spencer. He always gets quiet, and his sentences grow shorter when Spencer is mentioned.

"I'd better get back to work," I say.

"Good luck," says Nathan.

"See you later."

As I walk away, he watches Isaac swing back and forth. And he's still frowning.

Although more confusing than enlightening, my walk with Nathan and Isaac has woken me up. I'm ready to return to work on Spencer's novel with renewed vigour. There's a lot to be done before tomorrow. And not just to the manuscript.

I wish there were something to tip the balance of power in my favour with Spencer. If I were Paige, or Kayla, I'd think of something.

In the midst of these meditations, the phone rings.

"Dollface."

"Kayla. What's up?"

"I've got the bones of that gossip I was telling you about," Kayla says. "Six months ago I sold a duplex to a woman in the English department, Angie, an adjunct professor at the university, or assistant professor — something like that. This place would have been perfect for you. You could have rented the upstairs to cover the mortgage and —"

"*Kayla.*"

"Right. So Angie mentioned to me she was looking for a tenant. I said, 'Put the word out in the department.' She did, and you'll never guess who she took on as a tenant." She pauses for dramatic effect.

I bite. "Who?"

"A grad student."

"So?"

"Well, Angie's newish in town, out of the gossip loop. She didn't realize the grad student was Spencer's little love interest, the poet."

A moment's silence while I digest this. "Well, well, well."

"I think Angie's reaction was a little different when she found out what was happening."

"What was happening?"

"Angie's place has one of those old metal fire escapes around the back of the building. One night a couple of months ago, she heard a clanging and rattling. She thought it was a raccoon or something trying to get into the garbage pails.

"She grabbed a broom and went outside to scare away whatever it was that was making the racket. She was on her way around the side of the house when she realized the noise wasn't coming from an animal messing around in the garbage pails, it was coming from someone climbing the fire escape. So she stepped out of sight to see what was going on. What was going on was that Spencer was negotiating the fire escape, slipping into the poet's apartment through the back door."

I smile. The idea of Spencer scaling the fire escape is somehow heartening. What's the saying — the triumph of hope over experience? I'd like to see him in the grip of passion, gallivanting up and down metal stairs on the side of a house.

"Angie called me to find out what her liability is. If a faculty member breaks his neck committing adultery on your property, are you liable?"

"How can he carry on like this? Doesn't he know how small this town is?"

"Boys never think about the consequences of these things," Kayla says dismissively.

"Well, that's true — but up and down a colleague's fire escape?"

"I guess testosterone has its own take on reality. And he may not have known it was Angie's fire escape. I didn't get all the messy details. You know this town — the rectitude factor is suffocating. And there's more. It's all somewhat nebulous but apparently there was a muffled explosion at the university about ten years ago."

"A metaphorical explosion, right?"

"Metaphor, allegory — whatever, that's your area of expertise. All I hear is something went down, sparks flew. But it was very subdued. One wouldn't have noticed if one weren't looking for it,

I'm told."

"And this involved Spencer somehow?"

"Yes. How exactly isn't clear."

"I see." A moment passes while I puzzle over things. "God, Kayla, this is so tacky. I mean it's fascinating in a weird way — Spencer's life is sort of like a goofball soap opera. I keep phoning Morris hoping maybe he'll come back and hold Spencer's hand so I don't have to get involved, but there's no answer. Right now Spencer seems to be going along with the program, but then he'll dig his heels in. He could decide not to play at any minute. Just pull the rug out from under me. He's implied as much. I need some time out."

"No problemo, babe," she says. "See you in a couple of hours." And she's gone.

I sit for a while longer before tackling the manuscript again. How do I handle a guy like this?

I need a plan. Mother would know what to do. She always does. *Never wear white after Labour Day. A protein, a vegetable, and a starch each night for supper. Thank-you notes go to the hostess. You don't think it was the host who put the clean sheets on the bed, do you?* This was okay until I was twelve, when it became problematic, but there are times ...

If I were a character in Spencer's novel, this situation would afford me an opportunity to meditate on the venality of people, their moral corruption and shallowness. As his editor, I'd probably cut the passage. Too bad I can't cut real life the same way.

# Chapter 11

I SPEND SOME TIME going over the changes Spencer and I made today. When it occurs to me to glance at the clock, I realize Nathan's due any minute and I haven't the faintest idea what to feed him. I open the freezer and stand staring at its contents. As I'm debating whether to grill chicken or poach salmon, the doorbell rings.

I find Nathan standing in the courtyard, holding something bulky.

"Come on in." I stand to one side.

"Lasagne," he says simply as he steps over the threshold and hands me a large, heavy aluminium pan. He pulls off his jacket and drapes it abstractedly over a pile of coats and sweaters at one end of the sofa while he glances around. "I picked it up in case ..." His voice trails off. "It just needs to be heated." He pauses, then asks, apparently as an afterthought, "I hope you like lasagne."

"Love it. Especially when I don't have to cook it."

He follows me slowly up the stairs, glancing around at the exposed beams, the white walls, the open concept. "Nice place," he says. "Airy, and you must get lots of light."

I glance back at him sharply. Is he kidding? Apparently not; he has come to a halt on the middle of the first-floor landing and is looking around. Fortunately the lightbulb over the landing isn't working, or he'd realize he's standing in the middle of a perpetual blizzard of dust motes. Doesn't he notice the stairs are uneven? Doesn't he see the patchwork way the space is put together? The idiosyncratic carpentry, the wobbly walls? Oh well, I guess it does have a certain charm on first acquaintance. After all, its peculiarities weren't initially obvious to me, either.

"It must have been a coach house or something, originally," he says.

"I think it was the 'or something.'"

"How long have you been here?"

"A couple of years," I tell him. "We moved here after my husband and I separated." Might as well get the whole gruesome story out in the open right away. "My daughter Em and I. She's ten. Right now she's at her dad's while I try to whip Spencer's novel into shape." In the kitchen I turn on the oven and slip the lasagne into it. "Have a seat." I motion toward the table and chairs a few feet off to one side in the little alcove I've designated as the dining area — the table that, until just recently, Spencer and his oeuvre occupied. "Can I get you something to drink?"

"Do you have any coffee?" he asks, pulling out a chair and sitting down.

I brew a pot and carry it to the table, setting a cup down in front of him. "Milk? Sugar?" I slide the silver pitcher and sugar bowl, a wedding present from friends of my mother, toward him. I can't imagine what sort of lifestyle they envisioned for Jim and me. What could Mother have possibly told them that prompted them to give us such an outlandish gift?

Trying to appear nonchalant, I wait for the inevitable questions: *How long have you been separated? Do you have full custody?* In my limited experience (three dates), once a man finds out you have a history (an ex, a child), these first encounters usually become interrogations masquerading as dates. There are the standard pleasantries: *How do you do?* The initial tentative forays, *So, uh, how long were you married?* Then it gets down and dirty: *How many weekends a month do you have your daughter? Where does your ex live?* It's similar to a job interview, except if you're successful you don't end up with a job, you end up with a chance to go on a second date, usually just as nerve-wracking as the first — *How do you feel about ... hot tubs?*

But Nathan seems quite content to sit drinking coffee and examining his surroundings.

"Thanks for the lasagne," I venture.

"You're welcome," he says. "How's Spencer's book coming?"

The question catches me unprepared. To tell the truth or not? I open my mouth, then shut it again, probably resembling a fish plucked from the water left gasping on a river bank. What runs through my mind is: *friend or foe? Where do Nathan's loyalties lie?* If I tell him the book's a disaster, who will he tell? I don't want it widely known I'm reconstituting the book, since this will reflect badly on Spencer and might negatively affect sales.

"It — it — it's," I stutter, like a balky lawnmower trying to get started, "it's got potential. Yes." I nod. "Very interesting." Smiling brightly, I hop up. "I'll make a salad."

"Can I help?"

"Sure; here's some lettuce to wash."

While I'm busy reducing a tomato to a pile of mushy, toothpick-sized slivers and thinking, *Well, you killed that conversation in thirty-seven seconds flat — must be some kind of record,* the doorbell interrupts my interior monologue. For an instant I wonder who it can be, then I remember my invitation to Kayla — she's early.

"Shall I?" Nathan asks, tilting his head in the direction of the noise.

Considering the question, I stand for a moment, my knife hovering above the remains of the tomato. My indecision resolves the situation. "Um —" I begin, but Nathan has taken my hesitation as a "yes" and has gone to answer the door.

I hear the stairs protest as he descends, hear the door creak open and catch a snippet of "Happy Birthday" as it floats up the stairwell. Halfway through the first verse, "Happy birth —" Kayla stops short. "Hello, Nathan. Long time no see." He makes a murmured response I can't decipher, and she laughs warmly.

They know each other? I guess I shouldn't be surprised; Kayla is well connected. I'm mulling over the nature of their acquaintance — How did they meet? How long have they known one another? — when I hear someone coming purposefully up the stairs.

Resplendent in a shimmering yellow and orange silk outfit, Kayla crosses the floor, hands me a package and a bottle of wine and kisses me on the cheek.

"For me?" The package is wrapped in crinkly silver paper tied round with a red fabric ribbon.

"You're the birthday girl," Kayla grins.

I tear off the paper, tossing it to one side, and pull from the box something that resembles a flowery toque. "I am mystified," I say, holding the object aloft.

"It's a talking tea cozy," Kayla says. "Here's the timer, see? You punch in how long you want the tea to steep, push the start button, and —" she sets the timer for three seconds and shortly there's a burst of "I'm a Little Teapot." A perky computer voice declares "Tea's ready!" in a tone bordering on manic.

"How did I ever live without one?" I ask. "Thank you, Kayla. I'll treasure it."

"Happy birthday," she says. "Mmm, I smell food." By this time, Nathan has re-appeared and is poking around in the oven.

"I think it's almost ready," he says.

"I'll get the plates," Kayla volunteers, and there is a flurry of activity as she sets the table, Nathan shepherds the lasagne to the table and I finish assembling the salad. Finally we're seated at the table, plates piled high with lasagne and salad, wine sparkling in our glasses.

There's the usual interlude of small talk: *lovely weather, remarkable bank rates,* that sort of thing. Kayla and Nathan discuss the health of the real-estate market for a while. Nathan and I trade stories about the book world. Then Kayla asks, "How long have you two known each other?"

"We met Thursday," Nathan tells her.

"So what's up?" Kayla inquires vaguely.

"Elaine was just about to tell me what a dud Spencer Stone's novel is," Nathan says before I have a chance to answer. When I look up suddenly in his direction, he is occupying himself with a piece of lettuce, studiously avoiding meeting my startled glance.

"What?" I burst out. "I didn't say that."

"Well, it is," Nathan replies in a tone of calm decision, spearing the leaf. "A dud, a disaster, a literary catastrophe."

"How do *you* know?"

"Spencer has been shopping that thing around for years."

"Really?"

He nods, smiling wryly. "A friend of mine runs a small press on the West Coast. He read the entire manuscript two years ago, passed it on to me for my opinion. It was all very hush-hush because Spencer didn't want Hill to know he was thinking of jumping ship. My friend said he was tempted to take it on — Spencer's name practically guarantees sales — but it was so bad he had to send it back."

"Why doesn't Spencer just give up on it?" Kayla asks.

"Oh, he gets a lot of mileage out of it," Nathan replies. "Grants; it's good for his career; it's good for his stature at the university. 'I'm writing a novel' sounds much more impressive than 'I'm writing a short story.'"

"It isn't all bad." Even to my ears, my protest sounds unconvincing.

Nathan looks at me. "No?"

"That isn't what you told me yesterday," Kayla says. Under the table I give her ankle a short, sharp kick.

"Well, not an unmitigated horror."

"I'll grant you that," says Nathan. "I'm not a big fan of Spencer's, but he is capable of good writing sometimes."

"You just like the sex." I surprise myself by teasing him.

He shakes his head. "I like the musical elements, point and counterpoint."

"I cut out a lot of the music. It slowed things down."

"Leave it in and cut out the sex and you'll have a better book," he advises.

"Sex sells, music doesn't."

He nods thoughtfully. "You're right about that. I move a lot more *Story of O* through the store than books on Beethoven, or even biographies of rock stars."

"Okay, okay." I throw my hands up. "The truth is, the book is awful." I bite this last word out reluctantly, as if it is an admission of guilt.

Then it all spills forth: the full dreadfulness of the novel, the financial precariousness of the press, the need to keep Hill in the dark. ("Shouldn't be hard. He must spend a fair bit of time there already," Nathan observes. "Otherwise he wouldn't have become involved in this project in the first place.")

"On top of which," I add. "I sometimes get the paranoid feeling Jerri, our office-challenged receptionist, may have her eyes on my job."

"Jerri? The one who always cuts me off when she puts me on hold?" Kayla asks.

"That's the one."

"The mind boggles," Kayla says. "But surely Hill's not going to turf you and give her your job?"

"He let Morris walk."

"That's true." Kayla nods.

"And Hill wants to see first proofs in two weeks. On the other hand," I continue, "Spencer wasn't as awful today as I'd been led to believe. I have to admit I'm warming up to the guy —"

Nathan is suddenly wracked by a fit of coughing.

"Did something go down the wrong way?" I ask solicitously. He nods, reaching for a glass of water.

"As if you're any judge of character," Kayla says. She leans over to Nathan. "When it came to being faithful, her ex had the attention span of a gnat."

I shoot her a menacing glance. This is neither the time nor the place to get into a discussion of Jim's foibles, and especially not with Nathan. I barely know the man, and I don't want to revisit that part of my life right this minute.

"Anyway, that's what I'm devoting my week to, trying to salvage *Sound and Silence.*"

"Well, you might as well drink up and enjoy yourself tonight then." Kayla laughs, raising her glass. Nathan joins in, but his expression is hard to read.

A few minutes later he checks his watch. "I'd better get going," he says. "I've got to get Isaac to bed."

I walk downstairs with him and help him find his jacket. "Thanks for dinner," I say.

He smiles. "My pleasure. And happy birthday." Then he's gone, and the door shuts behind him with heavy finality.

I stand for a moment, puzzled. Aside from my initial anxiety, the evening started out relatively relaxed and cheerful, but at some point the atmosphere shifted; lightness shaded to something darker and more serious. I don't know what changed, or why.

As Kayla and I finish clearing away the dinner dishes, Kayla's cellphone rings.

"A client at 8:20 on a Saturday night — can you believe it?" She shakes her head, gathering up her purse and jacket. "I've got to go. Happy birthday, doll. Save me some cake. I'll try to drop in tomorrow." And she's out the door before I can ask her about Nathan.

Time to get back to work. I climb the stairs to the third floor, to the tangle of verbiage that awaits me.

I sit down and start in on the manuscript, but the sheets of paper slither through my fingers and onto the floor. I retrieve them, put them back in order and prepare to begin again. When I finally get down to work, the words slip and slide into meaninglessness, my concentration dissolves, and after twenty minutes of fruitless effort, I slump in my chair.

Something's bothering me, but what? Not the Spencer problem. That is causing me anxiety, no question, but this is a different sensation. Bubbles percolating inside me, slow and warm — curiosity about Nathan. I haven't felt them in a long time, not since Jim and I first met twelve years ago. (Okay, maybe once or twice since then, but it's been *years*. One year, at least.)

I always thought of myself as a pragmatist. I never thought in terms of falling in love at first sight or eyes locking across a crowded room. I assumed I'd meet a nice fellow, we'd date for a while, get to know each other, then decide on a mutually agreeable date and get married.

And for the most part, my first relationships followed that pattern, except for getting married. They were comfortable, pleasant and not very exciting. After my disastrous first year at university, I decided the academic life was not for me. I left school before the end of the final semester and found a job in a deli. Mother was not pleased; I deduced this from her terse letters. She took to writing these when I stopped answering the phone. I stopped answering the phone when she started yelling. I thought I'd let her get some perspective on the situation.

For the next few years, I travelled through the various circles of hell that constitute working in the Real World. I'd like to think the experiences built character, since they certainly didn't build a savings account.

After several years of this, I found work in a library. The change was like stepping from the din and chaos of a circus into the measured civility of a chamber ensemble performance. For the first few weeks on the job, I felt dizzy, disoriented. At any moment I expected the calm to be shattered. I expected to arrive at work one morning to find the building crowded with bustling people the way the offices had always bustled, sometimes with purpose, but more often without.

My duties included doing everything around the place except cataloguing books and setting board policy, tasks reserved for those who held degrees. I checked books in and out, shelved them, mended them and generally tried to protect them from the stresses of use. I helped patrons find answers to their questions, helped them find books ("Something romantic, but I don't like all that sexy stuff.") and gave them directions to the washrooms.

The moment I realized two years had come and gone since I had started to work at the library, I stopped to wonder if my life would always be so circumscribed. Would this be the rest of my life — working at the library, taking the occasional course in English lit at night school, drifting in and out of romantic involvements? On balance it didn't seem too bad, just flat. Then I remembered that *Casablanca* was showing at one of the revue houses that evening, and my anxieties assumed the weightlessness of irrelevance and evaporated.

I love movies. I love to sit in a darkened theatre watching larger-than-life, impossibly beautiful people do implausible things, and give myself over utterly to the fantasy. I'm not a member of the cognoscenti: I can't list all of Pasolini's work, don't know the name of Bergman's cinematographer. I have chosen to remain a happy amateur. I am content to meet each movie halfway, satisfied to be engaged, if not always challenged.

The night I first met Jim was rain-washed; mid-October's

deepening chill hinting at cooler temperatures to come. The sidewalk was slick with rain. In the street, traffic lights reflected off the shiny wash of water on the road's surface. Tree branches swayed in a breeze that sent leaves scuttling along the sidewalk. All in all, the evening was perfectly suited to the movie.

When the film ended, I emerged, satisfied and somnambulant, into the world of cars gliding along the street, the autumn smell of rotting leaves, the prick of rain on skin. Wandering through the front doors of the theatre and into the chill night air was like being rudely awakened. I stepped back and abruptly stepped on the foot of someone behind me.

I turned to apologize, and was held transfixed by the vivid blue eyes of a tall, slender young man who was grimacing and favouring his right foot.

He said something in reply, but I wasn't listening. There was something going on inside me, something sudden and unexpected. At the time, I identified the sensation as aftershocks of attraction. In retrospect, I think my internal alarm system was going off.

Now here it is twelve years later, and I'm not sure if those are alarm bells I'm hearing again. Could the bubbles of curiosity I'm feeling about Nathan be my wiser self's way of warning me off? Is it telling me, *Don't go there, girlfriend. You're just asking for trouble.*

I think of Nathan, the careful way he selects his words, his thoughtfulness evident in the book of stories he found me and the lasagne he brought. No, he's not my type. He doesn't have the dangerous glint in his eyes that Jim did, the one that promises — although I didn't understand it at the time — that my heart will be shredded into confetti. This sensation must be the result of a good dinner and a glass of wine — purely digestive.

I'm tidying up the manuscript, affixing a Post-it Note to the last page I worked on, when the phone rings.

"Hello?"

"Elaine." Paige's voice, bracing as a cold snap in February.

"Paige. How are you?"

"More to the point, how are *you?* I got your e-mails about Spencer Stone's manuscript. Sorry I couldn't get back to you sooner. One of our writers had a meltdown. Divorce, Revenue Canada and a major award all in one week. His circuits got a little over-loaded."

"I can sympathize," I say. "How have you been? We haven't talked for —" I pause, calculating.

"— three months," Paige finishes, almost without missing a beat.

"If you say so," I laugh.

"How's the manuscript coming?"

"I'm doing the best I can. This was supposed to be Morris's baby, but he bailed. Anyway, I keep plugging away at it, and it seems like Spencer is prepared to accept quite a few of my suggestions."

"That's good."

"Except he hasn't said for sure he'll accept them, and he's hinted he might not."

"Ah." She's silent for a while. "Let me give this some thought and I'll call you back."

"Okay. Thanks, Paige."

"Don't thank me yet."

# Chapter 12

SUNDAY

I'm up early. My shoulders ache, either from tension or from spending hours bent over Spencer's manuscript. I sit kneading the base of my neck, trying to figure out what to have for breakfast, when the phone rings.

"Emily and I had a perfect time yesterday," my mother announces without preamble. "The movie was sweet — no bad language, no sex, no violence. It's so rare these days. I was thinking I'd take her to lunch today, and then a museum. Care to join us?"

"Mother —"

"I know, I know, you're busy. Yesterday was the first time I've seen you in six months. Some people would be hurt if all their daughter could manage for a visit was an hour and a half every half year, but I understand. I was a working mother, too. So could you phone Emily's father and ask if she's available for lunch?"

"Sure, Mother. I'll get right on it."

"How's the work coming, by the way?"

"Kind of hard to tell. The editing's going fine; the book's pulling together really well. I just have to wait and see whether the writer will co-operate."

"I see," she says. Then, without missing a beat, "So you'll call James and get back to me." How does she manage to make a request sound like an order?

"Yes, I will, Mother."

As soon as I hang up, the phone rings again. "Elaine, I am not going to deal with that woman." It's Jim and he's not a happy camper.

"Let me take a wild guess," I say. "Mother."

"You got it," he says with barely concealed — in fact, not-at-all-concealed — irritation. "Your mother."

I sigh. "What happened?"

"I got to the theatre yesterday to pick up Em, and your mother reams me out for being five minutes late, then she starts in on my clothes, and after that it's why am I working as a house painter, don't I have any pride, what sort of role model am I for my daughter."

*How typical of Mother not to have mentioned this,* I think.

"I have to stand and take this in front of my child. I'm not doing her any more favours, Elaine. If she wants to see Em, you'll have to handle it. I'll drop Em off at your place, but I won't pick her up. I do not want to run into your mother."

"All right. Fair enough. Can you drop Em off here at noon? Mother wants to take her to lunch and a museum. I'll get her to drop Em off here when they're done and you can pick her up. How's that?"

"Fine." He sounds mildly conciliated.

"Good timing," Ed tells me when I get patched through to his and Mother's room. "She was just on her way to the pool."

"Mother," I say when she comes on the line. "Why are you making my life more difficult than it needs to be, especially right now?"

"I don't know what you're talking about."

"I just had a call from Jim. He says you took a strip out of him yesterday, and in front of Emily, too. You know better than that."

"He kept us waiting. And he looked like a bum. He should be ashamed walking around like that."

"Well, he's not ashamed, he's angry. I don't have the time to deal with this right now, and Jim's so ticked off he's not going to put up with any more nonsense." I can't believe I'm talking to her like this. "I calmed him down, and he said he'll drop Em off here at noon and you can pick her up. But if you want to see her after this, you will have to stop provoking him. I don't have time right now to run back and forth between you two."

"All right," Mother says, sounding slightly chastened. "I'll see you at noon."

Spencer shows up punctually at 10:00, relaxed and cheerful.

"Beautiful day, isn't it?" he says when I open the door.

I peer out. Sun, sky, the usual stuff. "Looks good," I say, thinking, *Let's get on with this.*

Work is going well, we're making good progress. In fact, I'm so caught up in the rhythm of work, I have to think for a second when the doorbell rings. Jim, I realize after a moment. With Em.

"Excuse me," I smile at Spencer.

I rush downstairs and find Jim, his bike propped against him, listening to something Em's telling him.

"Hello, Elaine. How's it going?" he asks when I open the door.

"Where's your car?"

"In the shop. Heater core. So Em and I walked. But I've got to get downtown." He indicates the bike.

"Sorry, I forgot. Spencer's here and we're plugging along. Come on up, Em. I'm working, so you'll have to wait quietly until Gram shows up, okay?"

"Sure, Mom."

"Thanks for dropping her off, Jim. I had a chat with Mother and told her to behave."

Jim rolls his eyes.

"It's the best I can do. Anyway, I'll ask her when she's going to drop off Em and I'll give you a call."

"Fine."

I park Emily in the living room with a book, but before I can get back to work, the doorbell rings again.

"Back in a moment," I tell Spencer. "Come on, Em."

I open the door, planning to pass Em to Mother and wave goodbye, but Mother elbows past me and heads upstairs.

"Mother," I protest. "I'm busy."

"I just want a glass of water, Elaine. You wouldn't refuse your mother a glass of water, would you?"

I follow in her wake and watch as she makes a beeline for the kitchen.

"How do you do?" She smiles at Spencer, who gives her a quizzical look. "I'm Elaine's mother."

I feel like curling up into a small ball and joining the herd of dust bunnies that congregates under the couch. From where I stand at the top of the stairs, I can see her casting a gimlet eye around, especially around Spencer, although he seems oblivious.

"Mother," I mouth silently. She waves her hand, dismissing me, and points at the glass of water, which she's sipping in a leisurely way.

Spencer glances my way. I smile then, and when his attention returns to the page in front of him, glare at Mother, who makes a noisy show of finishing the water.

"Must go," she warbles. "Emily? Ready to go?"

"Yup."

"Nice to meet you," Mother says to Spencer as she breezes past. "I'll have her back before 6:00, Elaine." Then she and Emily are down the stairs and out the door.

"My mother," I say to Spencer, feeling an explanation is necessary but unable to come up with anything more inspired.

"Evidently."


By the end of the day, we've dragged most of the story into the present tense and have pushed some of it out of our hero Sullivan's head, so the reader can draw a breath once in a while, look around and see some scenery. Still, I can't fight the suspicion we may not get this baby finished on time.

A few minutes before 5:00, Spencer glances at his watch and says, "I really must be going."

I'm ready for a break, but I want to pin Spencer down. "I think we've accomplished a lot today. How do you feel?"

"I think we're doing well," he says.

"Are you comfortable with the changes we've made?"

He gives me a long, level look. Then, without answering my question, asks, "Same time tomorrow?"

I'd like to push, insist on an answer, but I don't want to antagonize him. "Fine."

At 5:45, just as I'm debating whether to reheat some of last night's lasagne or make a sandwich, the doorbell rings. It's Mother returning Emily.

"So," she says, walking purposefully into the room. "This is the fellow you were so worried about. He seemed like a nice young man. What does he do?"

"He's a professor, Mother."

"That's not a bad job — regular hours, good benefits."

"He's married."

"Oh." Her disappointment is palpable. "And how did it go today?"

"I don't know. I can't get him to say whether he'll go along with the revisions."

"I don't see the problem," she says.

"I've edited, fixed it up, but I'm not sure he's going to agree to accept the changes I'm suggesting. The book will be a disaster if he doesn't, and my job may be down the tubes."

"Ah," my mother says. "So you have to sell him on your version of the book."

"Come again?"

"It's like my little old ladies, bless their hearts," she says, settling into one of the kitchen chairs. "They come in thinking they want one thing — to completely redecorate their homes, turn everything upside down. But I know better. They don't want that, not really — really they want something else. It would give them a heart attack to redo their houses. Do you have any idea how stressful it is to have your house turned inside out, to have strange men coming and going, to have projects running over budget?"

"What do little old ladies have to do with —"

"Listen, and don't interrupt. What my little old ladies really want is a bit of a change. They're bored, they want to have the fun of spending some money, they want to brighten the place up a bit, get some new knick-knacks their friends will notice and be jealous of. I go in, change the drapes, maybe reupholster a chair or two, put up new wallpaper or paint a wall, find them some tchotchkes — that's the easy part.

"The hard part is convincing them that it was their idea. They're just determined they want their houses overhauled. I convince them they're so shrewd to have saved all this money, outfoxed the overpriced designer and fooled their friends into thinking they've dropped a load of money."

This is how she talks about her clients, maternal with an undercurrent of edginess; the reverse of how she talks to me, edgy with a hint of maternal.

"I don't get the analogy," I say.

"It's simple, this guy —"

"Spencer —"

"Spencer? Who calls their kid Spencer? It sounds like some hoity-toity plate silver flatware pattern. Anyway, this Spencer is an author, so he wants to publish his book — whether he pretends differently or not. It's what authors do, publish. All they think about is getting published; it's their goal. This Spencer wants to publish — what you have to do is convince him he wants to publish the book your way. That's what you've got to sell him on."

"So I have to persuade Spencer that the book he really wants to publish is the one with my changes?"

"Persuade, convince — whatever buttons you have to push," she says offhandedly.

"Which buttons are we talking about?"

"Oh, the usual ones: pride, lust, greed. One of them ought to do the job. You'll figure it out."

"But what if I blow it?"

"Elaine, I don't see what you're so anxious about," she says with impatience. "It looks like a win-win situation to me."

Oh, she's been reading more of those self-improvement books again.

"Say you persuade him to accept the changes — the book goes, and everything's hunky-dory, right?"

"Uh-huh."

"What's the worst-case scenario? You can't persuade him, the book's a dud, you get fired, right?"

For some reason, this is not a comforting thought. "In fact, I get anxious now and then that the receptionist is gunning for my job," I allow reluctantly.

"I doubt it, dear. Who would want your job? But what I'm saying is, if you get fired, you can go out and get a real job," Mother crows. "One with benefits and a dental plan. Whatever you do, you'll do the right thing for you."

"Thanks for the vote of confidence."

"Don't thank me. Now, Emily," she says. "What would you like to do tomorrow?"

"I have school, Grammy."

"Of course you do. Well, maybe Ed and I can take you to dinner. How does that sound?"

"McDonald's?" Em says, taking advantage of this once-a-year opportunity. I never take her there.

"Sure."

"Great."

"Mother," I say. "I hate to put a wrench in the works, but you have to call Jim and sort things out with him. I don't have time to be a go-between right now."

She makes a face.

"Go on," I say, pushing a slip of paper at her. "Here's Jim's number. Give him a call, apologize. Be an adult."

"Oh, all right." Her hand darts out in a quick, jabbing motion and grabs the paper. On her way out, she pauses in the doorway and turns to me. "I'm sure you'll do fine with the book, Elaine," she says. And just for a moment, I feel oddly optimistic.

By 7:30 Em is back at Jim's and I'm back at my desk; by 8:00 I'm stumped. It's the beginning of a new chapter and Spencer's protagonist is mulling over life:

> The shift of sun on water threw layered reflections shimmering across the ceiling of his room. He stared at them, hoping to find the key that would help him translate those ephemeral hieroglyphs. Perhaps he could discover in them a pattern, an underlying structure, that would help him understand the incoherence his life had descended to.

What am I supposed to do with writing like this? It's all limp and mushy. Very few readers will be willing to wade through two hundred-plus pages of this sort of thing. *I* stare — at the wall in front of me. No shimmering layered reflections there, just drywall that needs painting.

I go back and read the end of the previous chapter. The narrative was moving along nicely before Spencer changed gears and stalled the whole thing.

The minutes tick by; my mind's a blank. I decide to do what I often do when I find myself at an impasse: clean the bathroom. The physical activity eases my jitters, and there's something satisfying about scrubbing a sink and watching the dirt wash away. A dusting of environmentally toxic cleanser, the sweep of a damp sponge, and once again the sink is pristine, the fixtures sparkle. The bathtub demands a bit more elbow grease, but the return for effort expended is considerable. Empty the wastebasket, vacuum the floor, and chaos is temporarily beaten back from one small corner of the world.

It is while I am thus engaged, bent over the toilet, my hands encased in yellow rubber gloves, the glow of physical exertion no doubt making my cheeks red and blotchy, my hair plastered to my forehead with sweat, that the doorbell rings.

*Of course,* I think. Whenever I look like a charlady, the doorbell is sure to ring. With my luck, it's the man of my dreams out there — an investment banker with a bruised heart and a healthy stock portfolio who just happened to get lost in my little town and unaccountably decided to ring my doorbell and ask for directions. *Yeah, right,* as Em says with a snort. More likely someone canvassing for the Cancer Society.

This is what I'm thinking when I open the door to find — "Nathan?"

A brief flash of apprehension tightens his forehead. Why are men always wearing apprehensive expressions around me? I've hardly said anything and this guy is looking worried.

"Elaine," he says blankly. He was maybe expecting someone else? This *is* where I live.

For a second we both stand in uncomfortable silence, then he's talking, his characteristic veneer of reserve melting as the words tumble out. "It wasn't when you first started working at the press," he says. "I'm not like that. I know myself well enough to realize that I'm not an impulsive person. It may have been the third or fourth time we ran into each other ..."

What *is* he talking about? I started at Hunter Press three and a bit years ago; I met Nathan (counting backwards) three days ago. Impulsive? What's that all about?

"... I think it was at the launch for that awful book of children's stories, *The Shining Mirror,* remember? How did Hill get snagged into that one? What happened with it, anyway — did it sell at all?"

"You're rambling, Nathan." But I'm beginning to smile, confusion and uncertainty ebbing.

"I realize that." He grins sheepishly.

"As a matter of fact, it sold about 500 copies out of a press run of 1,500, and we had, I think, about 450 returns. It did abysmally."

"Ah." Nathan nods.

"The woman who wrote it was big in storytelling circles, so Hill figured it would sell through there. But storytellers don't *buy* stories, they *tell* them."

"Oh." A pause. "Well, what I meant was, after the launch I was hoping to get to know you better. But then I found out you were married ..."

"Yes," I acknowledge. "I *was*." Emphasis on the past tense.

"And I, uh, you know, didn't think it was wise ..." his voice trails off. He examines a bit of fluff on his jacket sleeve with intense interest.

"I understand."

He shifts uneasily, looking up. "But then I heard you and your husband separated."

"Right." I nod. I'd like to help him out here, bridge the pauses, but I can't think of what to say. Suddenly all I can think of is how close he's standing.

"And then on Thursday you walked into my shop."

"Thursday," I echo. It seems months ago.

"Elaine." His tone changes, takes on urgency. "I'd really like to see you. You know, go out together, become acquainted." He paus-es. "But if you're not comfortable with this —" His voice is tight.

"Not uncomfortable, just surprised."

"Surprised," he repeats thoughtfully. "That's understandable, I guess," he continues after a while. "I haven't been pelting you with flowers or anything. That's not really my style."

"A good thing, too." I laugh. "I'd be uneasy getting pelted with flowers."

"You know what I mean," he replies. "What's the use of admir-ing someone from afar if you never do anything about it?" Irritation tinges his voice.

"You've been admiring me from afar?"

"Well, really since the first time we met, if I'm honest about it. But then I found out you were married, and I just can't, I mean, I've been —" he breaks off.

"What *is* your style, then, if it isn't flower-pelting?"

"Oh, God." He shakes his head. "It's been so long. I guess it falls into the mute-admiration category."

I laugh. "I'd love to get to know you better, Nathan. It's just that now is not a good time." I give him a quick rundown of how much work I've still got in front of me to get *Sound and Silence* fin-ished. "How about later, when all this has been sorted out? Can we get together then?"

He smiles. "I look forward to it."

I step outside. "Where's Isaac?" For the first time his absence registers.

"At a friend's house, watching TV. We don't have one, so it's a huge treat."

I hug myself against a cool breeze that's come up and realize I'm still wearing my clunky rubber gloves. Suddenly Nathan's hands are on my shoulders. Heat radiates from where he touches me.

"Elaine," he says, his tone serious. "Spencer, he's —" Nathan stops short, apparently debating what to say.

"I've heard the gossip," I say. "I've been warned. But to finish the book, I have to work with him. All I'm interested in is get-ting the edit finished and the manuscript off my desk — or my dining-room table, in this case — and out of my life."

He's silent for a moment, then he nods. "I see." We stand without talking for a few seconds. For an instant, it seems that he's about to say something, then his expression becomes unreadable and he draws away.

"I'd better get back to work," I say after a while.

"I'd better be going."

"Well."

"Well," he says. Then he turns and leaves.

*Oh, great. I've driven him off.* "Nathan," I start, but he's disappeared around the corner; the word floats unheard into the air. *Nice work, Elaine.*

What a nice man he is, thoughtful and concerned. Generous, too. It's been a while since anyone has looked out for me like that. For a long time I've been the one doing the looking out: first for Jim and Em, more recently just for Em. It's a nice feeling to know someone else has my interests at heart.

I'm about to run after him, but I stop. I have work to do, and not much time to do it. I could chuck the whole project, just give up and go after Nathan. It's a nice idea, but if I don't have anything to show Hill by Wednesday, I will also probably have no gainful employment shortly thereafter, which is not a nice idea.

I go inside and shut the door, but as I climb the stairs, what I'm thinking about is Nathan, and how he makes me feel. I try to give the sensation a name and to place when it was I felt it before. There was that rush of warmth, a bit of a sexual frisson, the thought, *Oh, that might be fun;* a sudden memory of body beside body, heat and closeness, the variety and complexity of textures one body comprises. But really, my response was composed of some other element.

*What is it?* I locate it in the carefully mediated way he approaches people; his quiet politeness, which can be missed if you're not listening for it; a carefulness that suggests that he has experienced loss or pain himself, and he does his best not to inflict them on others. I haven't entirely mastered this myself, still open my mouth at inopportune moments, but despite this deficiency in my own character, I appreciate it when I encounter it in others. I wonder what went wrong between him and his wife.

He seems like a reasonable person: intelligent, calm, with a sense of humour; not one to jump to conclusions or fly off the handle. If he were faced with problems in *his* marriage, my sense is that Nathan's the type who would stick it out and try to resolve differences, not the type to bolt. So, unless his ex-wife is a total wingnut, I don't understand why they came apart.

But if there is one thing I've learned, it is that no one standing outside a relationship can guess what makes it tick for the people inside it. Or stop ticking, for that matter. And sometimes it's a bit of a mystery even to those involved. This was made clear to me during a conversation Jim and I had at the Jitterbug Café last spring, when we met to discuss Em's spring break holidays.

The Jitterbug is one of two or three new coffee places that have appeared downtown in the last year. It is the darkest, therefore the kindest to wrinkling faces, and the neo-folk tunes on the sound system are kept at a reasonable volume. You don't have to shout to be heard.

Jim was hoping I'd say, *No problem, I'll take Em all week,* because he had a chance at a huge painting contract. I wanted him to split the time because the spring season in publishing is always hectic (we had nine books scheduled for release over the course of two months) and the rest of my life had gone down the drain the previous week. There was an unspoken tug-of-war going on.

"Is something bothering you?" Jim asked finally. "You're very cranky."

"I am not," I snapped, resentful he could read me so well. If he was out of my life, I wanted him to stay out of my head.

"Oh, really?"

"Okay, so I'm cranky." I toyed with my cappuccino spoon. "Steve and I called it quits last week." I hadn't even told Kayla yet that my second involvement in three years had fizzled to an awkward end. "I can't believe I'm telling you this."

Jim shrugged. "I already knew."

"How?" I demanded. I hadn't told anyone.

"Sasha heard it from Steve's secretary. Sasha's her massage therapist. But I don't think anyone else knows."

*Except the whole town,* I thought. "Well," I ventured presently. "Didn't it occur to you that it might be the reason I'm be a little out of sorts?"

"That was last week," he said. "I thought maybe since then your car broke or something."

"No, my car did not break. I am upset about Steve."

"Oh." Jim was silent for a moment. "Why?"

"Because I'd like to have a relationship that lasts longer than the trailers at the movie theatre. Since you and I broke up ..."

"I meant, why did you guys split up? I thought you got along well. And Em liked him."

I glanced around to see who was in earshot. Just some young hipsters pierced in the nose and ears and tattooed everywhere else, so young they probably couldn't conceive of Jim and me having sex lives. "I couldn't take the next step," I mumbled across the table to him.

He frowned. "What?"

"I couldn't get into bed with him."

*So that's what nonplussed looks like,* I remember thinking when I saw his reaction.

"Why?" he asked. "You didn't have any trouble with me."

It's true. It was a lot easier twelve years earlier. Life was simpler; my thighs were firm and I didn't considered Kraft Dinner a dietary staple — merely an occasional indulgence. Lovely bodies are wasted on the young.

"We walked all over town, then we went back to your place and went to bed," said Jim across the table.

"Cut to the chase, as usual."

"Well, it's true. We did."

I nodded nostalgically. "Yeah. We could do that then."

"You can still do it," Jim said. "You just need to take precautions."

"Maybe *you* can. Not me. That was pre-stretch marks, pre-postnatal potbelly."

"Give it a rest, Elaine. You're just feeling sorry for yourself."

"No, it's more than that. I guess the older I get, the stronger my sense of the ridiculous gets. The thought of undressing in front of a stranger cracks me up, and at the same time, it makes me feel like running screaming from the room. And anyway," I protested, "it's not as though I made a habit of jumping into bed with anyone who came along."

He grinned. "I know." Then he asked, "Out of curiosity, why did you?"

"Jump into bed with you?"

"Yes."

"Haven't we already had this conversation?" I didn't really want to go over this territory again.

"Not this specific one. We've had the one about how it happened — you breaking up with Ted, me breaking up with Anna. Then you turned the whole thing into one of the funny stories you haul out at parties: 'How I Met and Married a Penniless Philosopher.'" His voice is tinged with bitterness. "But I never asked you why it happened."

I thought back — the slap of cold air outside the theatre, the needles of rain on my face, and Jim — and I smiled. "I thought you looked sweet, hopping around like that. I thought, 'Here's someone who doesn't take himself too seriously. This could be fun.'" I looked at him. He looked away.

"And it was."

"Yup," he said shortly. His expression was difficult to decipher. "It was."

"For a while."

"A long while," he agreed.

"And then what, Jim?"

"What do you mean?" He looked up at me quickly, startled and slightly alarmed.

"When did it stop working for you?" The words burst out in a rush. The fights were over, we'd staked out our respective territories. We were friends now, the acrimony had shifted to mutual tolerance, even a bit of respect. I could ask this without provoking defensiveness. I could ask it and he knew I wasn't looking for a fight, just an answer. "I mean, it seemed to work fine for a long time."

Jim looked away, then down at his hands, which were busy

reducing a paper napkin to small, feathery shreds. "I'm not sure." He shook his head. "I guess when what we had stopped being what I wanted — after Em came and we were into the whole kid thing: family life, routine. Which isn't to say I knew what I wanted," he added. "But I thought I wanted something else, and I thought I might find it with someone else. So I started looking around." He gave me a wry grin, but his eyes were serious. "And you know what happened next."

We sat for a long time without talking. Then he picked up his spoon and considered it absently. "It would be nice to have some fun again, wouldn't it?" He caught the appalled look on my face and added quickly, "Not you and me. I don't mean it that way. It's just that everything seems so serious these days. Do you think it'll happen?"

A pause. "Yes," I said, realizing that I did think it would happen. For him, for me. "I do."

The things that keep us together, the things that blow us apart — relationships seem to be like Spencer's novel, works in progress, always under revision.

# Chapter 13

LATER, THOUGHTS OF NATHAN and Jim still lingering, while I'm considering having a bowl of cereal for Sunday dinner — too tired to fix anything fancier — Paige rings.

"How's it going with Spencer?" she asks.

"Fair to middling. He was here today. We worked on the novel and he left. I'm getting mixed messages from him — I'm suggesting pretty substantial changes to his book, and he's being evasive about whether he'll commit to them — but in other respects, he's been pretty reasonable."

"Don't be fooled," Paige says. "The man is a jerk."

I'm surprised by this forthrightness. Paige is honest to an almost ridiculous degree, but she makes a practice of being carefully neutral when she talks about people, especially anyone connected with the literary world. The circle she moves in, the community of writers and publishers, is a fairly small one. Since she never knows who might prove useful in future, she's at pains never to speak ill of anyone lest the comment make it back to the subject.

"I don't get it," I tell her. "I hear all this talk about how horrible Spencer is — and he *is* a bit prickly — but so far he's been reasonably well behaved with me."

"Don't be misled," Paige tells me. "The good behaviour is just a front. Partly it springs from his sense of self-importance, noblesse oblige — the elite being kind to the underlings. Partly it's a smoke screen to lure you into trusting him. Beneath that facade he's totally self-centred. A complete prick."

"Really?"

Paige sighs. "All right, Elaine. This isn't something I would normally disclose." She pauses for a beat, then the words tumble out rapidly, as if she's getting it all out as fast as she can. "When I was there at law school, a friend of mine got involved with him. I won't give you her name." She falls silent.

"And what?"

Almost reluctantly she continues, "She was pretty naive. Not blind, but inexperienced. He gave her a crash course in certain aspects of human behaviour. Spencer had her convinced he was going to leave his wife for her, that they'd go away together. She was devastated when she figured out what was happening. She was twenty-two — what did she know?"

"The explosion," I say. Something's bothering me, a nagging sensation, the same one I get when I'm trying to remember a person's name and it's just out of reach.

"Pardon?" says Paige.

I explain about Kayla's mention of a "muffled explosion."

"Oh, yes. There was an incident. She was upset, and made the mistake of mentioning their affair to a friend, a faculty member who worked in the Women's Studies department. The woman wanted her to go after Spencer, make a complaint to the administration. My friend thought about it, but she didn't really want the whole episode to take over her life. She just wanted to get out of there and to get on with things.

"So watch your back. If he sees an opening, he'll move in. Has he done his 'Let me not to the meeting of true minds admit impediment' number yet?"

"There's a passage in the novel —"

"Art mirroring life."

"I don't know. All I know is I have to get his book into print."

"Right. His book. He was working on it when she was involved with him. She never really thought he'd finish it. I'm amazed he let you have it."

I explain my kidnapping of the manuscript.

Paige laughs. "I wish I could have seen the expression on the guy's face. How bad is it?"

"It's way less bad than it was before I got my hands on it," I tell her. "It needs adjustments, but it's improving. It's just that he hasn't said he'll go along with the changes. He behaves as if he will, but, like I said, he hasn't given me a straight yes yet."

"No, and my guess is that he won't as long as he thinks he can get something out of the situation. The only way you're going to get a direct answer from him is if his cover is about to be blown and he's about to be revealed as the literary fraud he is."

"Which doesn't help me right now," I say. "He hasn't misbehaved with me —"

"Yet," interrupts Paige.

"— and it's not in my interests to publicize the fact that *Sound and Silence* is a bust. I'm the one who'll have to pay."

Paige is silent for a moment. "When's your deadline?"

"Spencer is due here tomorrow at 10:00. And Wednesday I've got to have either an explanation for Hill or a fully edited manuscript ready to go."

"Give me some time. I have an idea but I've got to sort some stuff out. I'll get back to you."

"Okay — and thanks, Paige."

What Paige has said has made me even more uncomfortable with Spencer. Time to call for reinforcements. I dial Kayla's number.

"I was just about to call you," she says when she picks up. "Bad news bulletin — two, in fact."

"What?"

"Morris is gone. According to his landlord, he packed up and left town. Apparently he had a lead on a job in the city. He told his landlord it was going to be good to have a life again."

I know how he feels. "What's number two?"

"I heard from Angie. The poet's out of the picture."

"What?"

"She turfed Spence out. Traded him in for another squeeze."

"The poet dumped Spencer?"

"You got it," Kayla says in a chipper tone.

"When?"

"A couple of weeks ago."

"Ow — that's got to hurt. If I weren't so irritated with him, I might almost feel sorry for him."

"Don't waste your sympathy. If he hadn't been playing out of school, it never would have happened. And if half the stories I hear about him are half true, he had it coming," says Kayla.

"Jeez, Kayla. No one has any secrets from you. What don't you know?"

"Well, I didn't know you've been seeing Nathan Marks."

"I haven't," I protest. "I met him for the first time on Thursday, like we told you."

A short bark of laughter. "That's so unlikely, it's probably true."

"What do you know about Nathan, Kayla?"

"He sells used books," she replies shortly.

"That's not what I mean."

"Oh, you want the dirt. Well, I sold him the house he owns. It dates from around the 1850s. The kitchen was added on in the 1950s. The cellar's a bit damp, but show me one in this town that isn't."

"*Kayla.*" *Yes,* I think, *I do want to know the dirt, so I can protect myself if I need to. No,* I think simultaneously, *I don't want to know the dirt. I don't want there to* be *any dirt. I want Nathan to be the easygoing, considerate man he seems to be.* I realize this is about as likely as being able to power my house with cold fusion, but that's how I feel.

"He and his wife bought the place when they first moved here — let me think — about fifteen years ago, when the market was really hot. She moved out eight years ago."

"Anything else?"

"She moved in with another woman. They bought a place further out of town and paid about $15,000 too much for it — real problems with the foundation. Two years ago, they split."

"You're holding out on me. Is Nathan a nice guy, or what?"

"Sweetie, *me* hold out on *you?* Never. As far as I can tell he's fine, but old Nathan plays his cards pretty close to his chest. You interested in him?"

"No, forget Nathan. All I'm interested in right now is getting this book out of my life. I need some kind of leverage to make Spencer go along with me."

"Sorry I can't help."

"I'm just not Machiavellian by nature. Spencer's going to be here at 10:00 tomorrow morning. Can you come over when Spencer and I are done? I need moral support."

She gives it a moment's thought. "Sure. I've got a showing, but I'll call Tony and see if he can cover for me."

"Thanks."

Instead of cereal, I open a can of soup, hoping it will give me a warm, fuzzy feeling. I carry it upstairs, settle down at my desk and get back to work. As I progress through the pages, I consider the situation. What to do about Spencer and the novel? What to do about Nathan? *What now?* I wonder. This question runs over and over in my mind, an uninvited, gate-crashing mantra, an album skipping (does that date me? do CDs skip?), an echo and its doppelgänger reflecting off each other indefinitely.

I wake up to the realization, *I'm waking up.* Oh, brilliant, Elaine. One of the most important nights in your life in recent memory (what does that say about my life of late?), and *you fall asleep.* You don't even have the sense to have a precognitive dream forecasting how to sort everything out. That was the least you could do.

On top of which, I fell asleep face down on Spencer's manuscript, so I awake to discover my left eyeball's squashed out of alignment and half the room is a fuzzy blur.

What time is it? Squinch the left eye shut, focus the right: 12:35. The last time I checked, it was around eight. Well, that's just dandy. Four hours erased from an already crowded schedule.

Let's see, I figure there are twenty hours' more work to do on the manuscript. So, a cup of coffee, a slice of bread, and thou, Spencer, beneath the sagging ceiling joists. At this point, the work proceeds fairly quickly because what has gone before determines what will follow. I'm having so much fun that before I know it, it's 3:30 a.m.

Time to get some sleep. I have to be in top form tomorrow, light on my feet and ready to out-manoeuvre Spencer.

Monday morning, still dark out. Peer at the clock: 6:37. After three hours of bad sleep, time spent mostly tossing and turning, I'm awake — barely — and alive, but I'm not happy about it. Although the alternative is less attractive.

I have roughly three hours to get some work done before Spencer shows up. Fire up the coffee maker, leave a message for Jerri, turn on the computer and get down to work.

As I sit in front of the monitor and scroll through Spencer's prose, I wake up more completely by degrees. I print off the last chapter I've been working on, and, as often happens while reading hard copy, details that weren't as obvious on screen begin to register, scenes and passages of dialogue catch my attention. And gradually, inexorably, a realization dawns on me. One passage catches my eye:

> "'Let me not to the meeting of true minds admit impediment,'" he said.
>
> "Shakespeare," she replied.
>
> He reached for her, hungry for the feel of her, the smell of her. She pulled away.
>
> "What about your wife?" she asked. A shadow hid her face, obscuring her expression.
>
> "Louise?"
>
> "Yes."
>
> "What about her?" Why was she drawing Louise into this? Why, by speaking his wife's name, by evoking her image, did she bring Louise between them? This should have been their time together, alone, just the two of them. It was enough for him to be here, with her. Wasn't it enough for her? Didn't she understand how short this time was, how rare?
>
> "What will you tell her?"
>
> There was — there had always been, he saw now, something cold and implacable at her core, something hard, judgmental and unyielding —

We get it, Spencer, we get it. She's no push-over.

And that's the moment when what's been staring me in the face for three days suddenly clicks into focus. I lean back and rub my eyes. Sullivan *is* Spencer, despite my earlier reluctance to see it. If this is so, why has Spencer made Sullivan so unsympathetic? Who in their right mind would put himself down on paper so revealingly, all the incriminating evidence in plain sight, without one redeeming characteristic?

The answer comes to me with a jolt: Spencer doesn't realize how truly unlikeable Sullivan is. Spencer simply has no perspective — he thinks Sullivan's a nice guy, just hard done by.

My immediate impulse is to push away the manuscript. But I can't. And this interesting development means there's the question of libel; I'm going to have to go back over the book and see who, besides Spencer, makes an appearance in these pages. There is not one iota of salacious curiosity at work in this; it's a small town and I simply have to make sure there's nothing in here that might be actionable. It's my responsibility.

Seven pages later, I'm trying to decide whether one of the more vacuous characters in the book represents Spencer's attempt to settle a score with a local newspaper critic, when the phone rings.

"Hello?"

"Hi?" It's Jerri at the other end. I recognize the rising intonation which turns every statement into a question. I wait to see if she's going to let me in on the reason for the call. After a silence of several seconds, I give in.

"Yes, Jerri?"

"I remembered. It wasn't Crystal the other day, it was Bristol."

"Bristol? The printers? The printers called?"

"I guess so."

"It must have been Ghislaine. What did she want?"

"For you to call her."

She's doing this to make me crazy, I know she is. "Do you remember what it was about?"

"Um, something about *Highways and Byways* and photos."

"Did they get the photos?"

"Dunno." She gives the matter some thought. "Want me to call them?"

"Yes, I do. I want you to call Ghislaine and ask if she got the photos. They can't print the book without the photos and scans. Her number is in the Rolodex on my desk under 'Bristol.' If they haven't received the package yet, you'll have to call the courier and find out where it is."

"'Kay."

"And then call me back and let me know what's happening, all right, Jerri?"

"Got it."

I mentally walk through last Wednesday morning when I prepared the package and handed it to Jerri. I gave her the original photos that will illustrate *Highways and Byways* and their scans, labelled, in an envelope, ready to be sent. All Jerri had to do was slip the package into a courier's envelope, copy the address from the front of the package I gave her onto the mailing label and hand it to the courier. I'd already walked her through the process when we sent off the final pages, so I assumed she could handle this fairly simple transaction — apparently I assumed wrong. A delay of five or six working days means we'll have lost our place in the print lineup, which means further delays.

There were about thirty original photos painstakingly gathered from the authors, the archives, meticulously scanned, all in order, credits noted. To start the whole process again at this date ... It's a good thing I'm not at the office, or I'd eat her alive.

Right now, though, Spencer takes priority. I print out last night's work, and just as I've finished getting everything organized on the kitchen table, the doorbell rings. Spencer. I wave him inside and linger for a moment or two, hoping to see Kayla's little car come scooting down the laneway. Where is she?

Upstairs I find him already seated at the table, pulling out the revisions I gave him yesterday. I assess him discreetly; he doesn't look like someone who recently got dumped by his romantic interest. We swap stacks of paper and get to work.

Within a few minutes, Spencer seems completely immersed in the task at hand, working steadily through the pages in front of him. He stops occasionally to cross out a word or make a note. I read through the material he has returned, noting the changes he's accepted, reading the comments he's scribbled into the margins.

We've been working for about half an hour when the phone rings, shattering the silence. I hop up to answer it.

"Hello?"

"Elaine." It's Paige.

"Hi —" I start. Then I stop. There sits Spencer. "Uh ... hi."

"It's Paige," she says, sounding slightly miffed by my low-key response.

"I know."

"You sound odd. What's wrong?" Then, an instant later, before I can think of how to frame a response without letting Spencer know we're talking about him. "Ah ... is Spencer there now?"

"Absolutely," I say. "No question about it."

"Can't talk?"

"Well, I'm right in the middle of something. Now's not a good time. How about later?"

"I've got a few suggestions to run past you. When's good?"

"In a couple of hours?" I'll be able to take the call on the upstairs extension, out of earshot.

"Right. Talk later, Elaine." I sit back down to work and gradually the rhythm of work takes over. I get involved in the dialogue taking place between Spencer and me in the pages of the typescript. I propose changes; he agrees or counters with another suggestion. And so it goes for fifty pages.

We've been working for close to an hour, maybe longer, when I recognize the sensations in my mid-section for what they are: not rumblings of anxiety, but pangs of hunger. Of course — it's late morning and I haven't had breakfast yet, only infusions of caffeine. I get up and start rummaging around in the kitchen searching for carbohydrates, which are always most effective at filling the void.

While I'm poking around in the cupboard over the sink, I catch the tail end of something Spencer is saying. "... I really appreciate it."

"Pardon?" I peek around the cupboard door.

He's leaning back in his chair and appears as jolly as I suspect he is capable of appearing. In this case, it means he's twirling a pencil and looking slightly less self-conscious than usual.

"I said, it's kind of you to spend so much time on this. I'm sure you have a few other things to do."

*Just a few, and they're minor, really: hunt, gather, cook, clean, keep the household from falling apart completely.* "Oh, that's all right," I duck back inside the cupboard. "Hill's got the project on a pretty tight schedule." *Where is the loaf of bread I bought on Thursday night?*

"I really appreciate it."

*Why is he going on about this?* "Yes, well, you know the saying: 'Desperate times call for desperate measures.'" I shut the cupboard door. "Do you want something to eat?"

"What? No thank you."

I settle for Pop Tarts and jam two into the toaster.

"It's been a pleasure getting to know you, Elaine."

*Only because I am a paragon of self-control.* "Coffee?" I offer.

"Please."

While I rattle around in the kitchen for a few minutes more, waiting for the Tarts to toast, I fill the coffeepot with water and am about to empty it into the reservoir, when I become aware of a nearly inaudible sound.

With a start, I realize Spencer is standing right behind me; his hands rest lightly on my shoulders. I jump, spraying water all over the counter and floor.

"I didn't mean to surprise you," Spencer says.

"*Surprise* me —" Surprise is a dozen long-stemmed roses, a box of Belgian chocolates; surprise is nice. This isn't surprise — this is creepy.

"In fact," he interrupts, his hands nudging me around to face him, "we get on remarkably well."

My pants are wet and cold where the water spilled on them and they're sticking to my legs. I can feel the water soaking into my socks. I hate having clammy feet.

"We're good together, aren't we, Elaine?" His voice is low, seductive. His hands slip to my waist, he pulls me closer.

I wedge the half-empty coffeepot between us. "Pardon?"

"Come on, Elaine, I know how you feel about me. Why else would you set it up this way — you and me, alone together at your place?" He tries to ease the coffeepot out of the way, but I hold it tight. "If anyone understands me, you do. You know how difficult it is to be a writer, the deep loneliness —"

"— 'this deep loneliness, this gaping emptiness that yawned within, a stark landscape of absence,'" I push him away. "You're kidding, right? You can't be serious. You're plagiarizing yourself — although I'm not sure if it's plagiarism when you're stealing from yourself." The words spill out in a frantic rush. We face one another across the tiny kitchen.

Spencer glares at me, eyes narrowed. "What do you mean?"

"It's in there —" I wave at the piles of paper on the kitchen table. "Around page 180, when Sullivan's putting the moves on what's her name — Audrey, the librarian. Go ahead, check it out and see."

He ignores this remark. For the space of a breath, he stands rooted to the floor, then he advances a step. Instinctively, I retreat — except there's nowhere to go. The kitchen counter is digging rather painfully into my lower back. After a moment, he seems to reconsider and leans back against the refrigerator.

"What's your little game, Elaine?" he asks lightly. "What is this all about?"

"I don't play those kinds of games, Spencer. This is about me trying to salvage your book."

His expression shifts. His voice becomes dangerously calm; a warning glint sparkles in his eyes. "What do you mean *salvage?* We've only been tightening it up. You said so yourself. *Minor changes, a little shaping,* is what you said. It doesn't need *salvaging.*"

It's like slamming into a brick wall, understanding suddenly that Spencer really has no idea how bad his book is.

"Spencer, your book is a disaster," I say. My job is already down the tubes at this point I figure, so there's nothing left to lose. I might as well tell him the truth. "It's overwritten, it's self-indulgent, it's boring —"

"Who are you —" He straightens. "— you — you're nobody to tell me —" Anger renders him incoherent.

He turns away, starts gathering up papers from the kitchen table and jamming them into his briefcase.

"What are you doing?"

"Taking my book — my *disastrous* book," he sneers, "and leaving. I'll be speaking to Hill. We'll see if you have a job after this."

Then he's gone, storming down the stairs.

After a moment's hesitation, I follow him. If I can just catch up to him, maybe talk to him, I might be able to calm him down, convince him to come back and finish the edit.

I make it downstairs just in time to see Spencer's car speed down the driveway and disappear around the corner.

"What gives?" I turn to find Kayla staring wide-eyed after the departing Spencer. "Sorry I'm late, babe. Tony couldn't make it right away, but it looks as though you've taken care of business all on your own. What was that all about?"

I sag against the door frame. "That was my job driving away."

# Chapter 14

"TELL ME ABOUT IT," Kayla says.

I give her a quick run down. Five minutes later I finish, "So I blew it."

"No." Kayla shakes her head. "You did the right thing. What else could you do?" She pats my hand.

"Thanks. But what about my job?"

"Job, schmob. Come work in my office. You can write sales copy for the newspaper listings. You've got all those lovely adjectives at your fingertips, right? I mean, *charming* gets old. We're drowning in *charming* houses. *Lovely. Mint.* You'll be a breath of fresh air."

I laugh. "Right. *Evocative two-bedroom bungalow. Lots of latency. Prosaic split-level. Suitable for large domesticated groups.*"

"What did I tell you? The buyers will be fighting tooth and nail."

"Thanks, Kayla." But we both know the offer's not serious.

She has picked up making coffee where I left off and is spooning grounds into the coffee maker. I slump wearily into a chair and sit, considering the various possibilities. A few minutes later she sets a steaming mug in front of me.

"It's your call, babe." She sits down beside me.

"What I really want is to keep my job, but we both know that's not going to happen."

Kayla says, "Speaking of jobs, I should really go give Tony a break. You all right on your own?"

"I'm fine." And it's true, I am. A bit drained, a bit sad, but basically less anxious than I would have anticipated. "I'm just going to do some math and see what the future holds."

She gives me a hug. "I'll drop over later. We can do dinner."
*Now what?*

Is that the end of it? Is my time at Hunter Press over? If Spencer is as good as his word — though there's reason to doubt that — and he complains to Hill, I'm toast. It may be time to update the old resume.

And while I'm in worry mode, what about Nathan? I like him, but do I want to risk getting involved when such a major part of my life is so uncertain? Doubts about my job coupled with the anxiety of starting a new relationship — my whole life could turn into one big worry-fest. Something to look forward to.

It might work out between me and Nathan, but there's the chance it might not, and I'd find myself in the not too distant future asking myself the very same question that popped into my head right after Jim and I decided to call it definite, permanent, uncategorical, unequivocal quits — *Now what?*

I can see the end of my marriage as stages now. There had been the opening volley with the pyrotechnics about Viv at Chez Nous, then we had the sexy lingerie interlude, followed by the Peggy contretemps. Our exchange concerning Peggy took place in a grocery store, as have so many pivotal experiences in my life. Initially Jim denied the charge, but in the frozen desserts section he admitted he'd been equivocating. "So you *have* been seeing someone," I hissed as we rolled up to the baking section. In the vicinity of the eggs, he allowed as how, yes, he had been seeing someone, a secretary in the admissions office, to be exact, but he wasn't sure how serious it was.

"Serious?" I spat out. "Serious? *Marriage* is serious; *parenthood* is serious. Philandering isn't serious — it's self-indulgence."

"Elaine," he breathed, in a patient tone.

"Don't 'Elaine' me," I snapped, slamming a carton of eggs into the cart with such force I cracked two of them.

A week after the supermarket exchange, Jim and I sat at the kitchen table. *Our* kitchen table, soon to become solely *my* kitchen table. It was a heavy ungainly affair, pieced together from scraps of a barn door, scarred and scratched and given to popping apart at inopportune moments.

At that table Em learned to eat with a spoon, made her first forays into the visual arts (these creations were given pride of place on the front of the refrigerator, already crowded with magnetic letters of the alphabet) and learned to write her name. And on that washed-out January day, the table stretched between Jim and me, an unbearable expanse.

"What do you want to do?" he asked. The Peggy explosion was old news, the dust had settled.

"Emerge with my self-respect intact." (Kayla had been coaching me.)

"I'll call Peggy and tell her I can't see her anymore," he said.

I shook my head. "If it isn't Peggy, it'll be someone else. We've been through this already. I don't think there's a lot to be gained by going over the same old stuff. I'll get angry, you'll get defensive; nothing will get resolved."

Jim nodded. "You're probably right." He looked worn out, and his weariness coupled with the resignation in his voice made me want to cry. We had worked so hard. How had it come to this?

When I picked Em up from the after-school program later that day, I tried to break the news to her gently. "Dad's going to go away for a while," I told her.

But she was way ahead of me. "You guys are breaking up, aren't you? Like Sheila's mom and dad." Her best friend's parents — Glenn and Shelley McKay — had come unglued in a blaze of incendiary fights. Em had watched the process, fascinated.

I winced. "Not quite like that, but along those lines."

"Why? Dad cooks dinner sometimes, and washes the dishes, too."

Division of Labour had been one of the flash points in the McKays' relationship.

"Yes, he does," I allowed, not wanting to take any credit from Jim. "But cooking dinner and washing the dishes aren't the whole story. People grow and change. Sometimes the changes bring them closer together, sometimes they push them further apart." *Why does it sound as though I'm discussing magnets?* I wondered.

"So you and Daddy got pushed apart?"

"I'm afraid so, sweetie."

*Now what,* I thought later when she was in bed, while I sat at the kitchen table. *And when is now? We must be into post-marital.*

I felt desolate — alone, empty, tired. Jim was sleeping at our friends' house. Tomorrow he would be coming to pick up his clothes. Even though I had asked him to leave — as Em is so quick to point out — it was difficult not to feel abandoned. If Jim hadn't in fact abandoned me, he had abandoned some idea of family that we had shared.

I don't want to go through that again. I don't want to sit alone contemplating the rubble of a failed relationship. I guess that's part of what prompts me to keep Nathan at a safe distance. I know it's a bad strategy to withdraw rather than be hurt. Follow that course of action and life in a plastic bubble is the only option. But there are enough changes in my life right now. I don't need any more.

I pick up a page from *Sound and Silence* off the floor and find a pencil beside the phone. Then I start to make a stab at calculating how I'll manage to squeeze my current lifestyle out of unemployment — or in the current new-speak, employment — insurance. Fewer trips to the hairdressers (at least I won't have to field as many artfully phrased questions like, "Wouldn't a henna rinse make a nice change?"), fewer visits to the dentist (which reminds me: I have to get him to check that upper-right rear molar that always twinges when I eat ice cream), get those library books back on time and quit socking money into a retirement fund — if I'm not working, what's to retire from?

My thoughts are interrupted by the phone ringing. Maybe it's a telemarketer trying to sell me something. I could ask what that kind of work is like — it might be a line of work worth investigating.

"Hello?"

"You sound glum." Paige's voice.

"Yeah, Spencer's on the warpath. He made a move on me and I lost it; told him what I really thought of his book."

"Really?" A hint of amusement warms her voice. "Well, I've been thinking —"

"Listen, I don't think there's any point in pursuing this," I say. "My sense is, I'm dead in the water."

"You may be right," she says in her characteristically blunt fashion.

*You don't have to agree quite so quickly,* I say to myself.

"But let's not discount Spencer's ego," she continues. "He has a lot invested in this book, in getting it published and being seen to be a novelist. He's been toting that thing around for years. Decades, to be accurate. Let me just run a couple of points past you ..."

When I say goodbye to Paige several minutes later, it is with a lighter heart. The sense of defeat that settled in after this morning's debacle has lifted a little. The worst is not over yet, but I can imagine it being over.


I have a plan. Bearing in mind Mother's comments and Paige's suggestions, I dial the office.

"Hunter Press?" Jerri answers.

"Jerri, it's Elaine. Where's Hill?"

"In the conference room, working on that biography? I can't put you through to him. He's told me to hold his calls."

"Has Spencer called or showed up?"

"Spencer? No."

"Here's the deal," I say. "If Spencer shows up, put him in Hill's office. Don't tell Hill he's there. I'm on my way. Got it?" I hope some of this will stick.

"Spencer goes in Hill's office. You're on your way."

"Good. But don't tell Spencer I'm on my way, okay? Just let him think he's waiting for Hill."

"Got it."


Ten minutes later, I rush into the office. Jerri exhales with relief when she sees me. "Is Spencer here?" I ask.

"Yeah."

"Is he in Hill's office?"

Her head bounces up and down like one of those bobble-head dogs I occasionally see in the rear window of cars. "He's really angry," she whispers, clearly relishing the drama of the situation.

"What's going on with Bristol?" I ask as I hurry past her desk.

Jerri shrugs, shakes her head, hands in the air. "No idea" says the expression on her face, but I can't stop now to discuss it with her.

In Hill's office I find Spencer pacing back and forth in front of Hill's desk.

"What are you doing here?" he spits out.

I shut the door. "About this morning," I say.

"What about it? You were completely out of line to speak about my work that way."

*Who* was out of line, buddy? I'm tempted to clarify this point, but I'm thinking of what Paige said: *be cool, calm, in control.* I'm thinking *be strategic,* I'm thinking *don't blow it.* "I'm sorry you feel that way, Mr. Stone. I just want you to know, if Hill gets wind of how you feel, he'll probably take me off the project."

"I would hope so. I can't possibly work with you anymore. Not after what you said. Your behaviour was completely unprofessional."

I let that last hit pass, concentrating on my plan of attack. "He'll need to find somebody else to do the edit, somebody more congenial."

"That goes without saying," Spencer nonetheless says.

"I'm sure he won't have any trouble finding someone who would want to work with a writer of your reputation. It would be a real feather in that person's cap. Of course, at this late date, Hill will have to get a freelancer — there's no one else at the press right now but me. Freelancers," I sigh. "They have no loyalty, there's no threat they'll lose their job. I wonder how long before people would start to ask how well you can really write ..." I give him time to imagine gossip springing like an energetic frog from one person to the next. I'm going to walk him through all the ramifications of what may follow step by step, as Paige suggested. "On the other hand, maybe Hill will do the edit himself."

"Hill?" says Spencer sharply. Obviously this possibility hadn't occurred to him.

"An important book like yours, that's probably the likeliest scenario." Another pause. "I wouldn't call Hill patient or easygoing ..."

Spencer is silent, considering this possibility.

I'm thinking about what Mother said: *pride, lust, greed* — one of them has got to work, although I would rather avoid pushing the lust button. Let's go for pride. "Of course," I continue. "At this late date, Hill might just decide to can the project entirely. That's always a possibility. Better not to publish than to put out a less than perfect book. You yourself made a similar point."

"That's true," Spencer allows.

"But it's been in our catalogue. The campus bookstore has quite a large order in. It would be too bad to disappoint people." I can hear him considering this option: the novel-less novelist. All the whispers, all the buildup, all the chat on campus, words dropped here and there, to colleagues, in class — *Yes,* a humble smile. *My novel is scheduled to come out this fall.* — all the sound and fury signifying what, if the book doesn't come out?

"I, on the other hand, would have no inclination or incentive to discuss the *minor changes* made to your book."

I can almost hear the gears turning. Finally, Spencer says, "They *were* minor, weren't they?" A little of his old confidence is sneaking back in.

"*Very* minor," I allow. "Although" — I don't want him to think he's home free — "there are more minor changes that still need to be made."

"How soon do they have to be made?"

I take a deep breath. "By Wednesday."

"That's only two days —" he starts to protest.

Now for my trump card. "A friend of mine — possibly you know her? Paige Turner — Paige said if I thought it was a good idea, she'd be prepared to consider running an excerpt of *Sound and Silence* in *City* magazine."

"Paige Turner? She did?"

"An excerpt in a national magazine of that calibre could probably bump sales up several thousand copies. You may not be interested in sales, but with numbers like that, you'd be on the best-seller lists, where you'd catch people's attention, critics' attention — the attention of people who nominate books for awards."

Spencer says nothing.

"Contingent on my approval, of course."

"Ah."

"I'm hoping to be in your acknowledgements, you know. *Special thanks to Elaine Salter for her eagle editorial eye,* something like that."

"That's it?" Spencer asks. "That's all? You're not going to demand half the prize money when I win the Booker?" He chuckles, trying for lightness and humour, although the undercurrent of unease is still there.

"That, and a promise of professional behaviour on your part. You'll get your advance against royalties once the edit is finished, but that's the only advance I'm willing to tolerate."

"And Paige will do this only on your approval?"

"Only on my approval."

He thinks for a moment. "Can you give me a couple of minutes? I have to make some phone calls, reschedule some meetings."

"Fine."

# Chapter 15

I PEEK INTO THE CONFERENCE ROOM. "Can Spencer and I work in your office?" I ask Hill. There's no way I'm going to let Spencer back into my house. Even if he has promised, more or less, to behave.

Hill looks up from the vast oak table, which is littered with piles of paper, post-notes and coffee cups. His eyes are red-rimmed. He runs his hand thoughtfully through his dishevelled hair.

"Sure. How's it going?"

"It's coming along."

"More than I can say for this." He waves his hand over the table. "Yeah, go ahead. I'll look in after lunch."

"Could you wait until Wednesday?" I ask. "The book is just pulling together. I don't want to lose focus. By then it should all be sorted out."

"Wednesday it is," he says, scribbling on a Post-it Note and sticking it onto the page in front of him. Once I get Spencer settled, I pop out to find out from Jerri what's going on with Bristol. "Any news?"

"Well, the coffee maker exploded this morning, but I don't think that's what you mean."

"No. You're right, I don't, although I'm sorry to hear it." I imagine the wall of the staff room splattered with coffee. Poor Janine, all alone in the office with Jerri. She should get danger pay. "What I meant was, what's the situation with Bristol?"

"The courier put a tracer on it, and they say the package is in Edmonton."

"Edmonton?" I burst out. *Take a deep breath,* I tell myself. Take ten. Better yet, take none, pass out and maybe all this will clear up by the time you regain consciousness. "What's it doing in Edmonton?" I ask, struggling to keep the mounting anger out of my voice. "It was supposed to go to Quebec. Edmonton is in exactly the wrong direction."

"They think it got wedged between two big packages that were going to Edmonton."

"When did they tell you this?"

"This morning, after you called."

"Have you heard from them since then?"

"No."

"Give them a call and find out what's happening. We're low on their list of priorities. We can't sit around waiting for them to call us. Find out where it is and when Ghislaine will get it. Please," I add, not wanting to sound like Mother.

"Rightee-o."

Spencer begs off at 3:30 for a meeting he couldn't postpone, which is fine with me. I've spent so much time with the characters in his book — and a needy, demanding bunch they are, too — that I'm ready to strangle them. I've been back and forth through the novel so repeatedly that it's all turning to mush. I suspect any work I'd do at this point would do more harm than good. We agree to meet again, at the press, at 9:00 the next morning. On my way out I check with Jerri, who hasn't heard anything new from the courier. Then I decide to head home.

I'm surprised to find Mother waiting by my front door. "I phoned the office and they said you'd just left, so I decided to meet you here."

Something's bothering her. I can tell by the way she's fidgeting with the clasp on her purse.

"Come on in."

Upstairs I offer her something to drink. "Coffee? Tea?"

"No, no." She shakes her head briskly. "I want you to phone James and ask when he'll drop off Emily. She and I decided we'd go to the art gallery after school today."

"Oh, no, Mother. I'm not getting stuck in the middle of this. You're going to call Jim yourself."

She draws herself up to her full haughty height of five-foot-nothing in three-inch heels. "I'd appreciate it if you'd call."

I sit down across the table from her. "I've already explained. I am not calling Jim. You have to sort this out with him." I can't believe I'm talking to her this way, the way I talk to Em, the way Em talks to me sometimes.

"I can't call him."

"Then you won't see Em."

Her chin juts pugnaciously.

"Look, Mother, even if I had the time to deal with this right now, which I don't, you've got to handle it yourself. If Jim and I can work things out, more or less, you can too. He's the father of your granddaughter, and you need to have a civil relationship with him."

She deflates, crumpling a little. "That's what Ed said."

"Ed's a smart man," I say. "This isn't about you. It's about Em. She loves her dad, and she loves you. How do you think she feels when you're rude to Jim?"

"Oh, all right," she snaps. "Where's your phone?"

"On the desk."

She marches over, punches angrily at the buttons, then returns to tell me, "I got his answering machine."

"Par for the course. Sit down, have a cup of coffee. Wait a little while. Maybe he'll call back."

We talk for a while. I tell her how things stand with Spencer; she tells me how The Group is doing. She tells me she and Ed are planning a trip to Florida during the winter, then lets drop she had a health scare a few months ago, a cardiac arrhythmia.

"Why didn't you tell me?" I demand.

"Ed thought I should but —" she shrugs. "I had some tests. Nothing showed up, and then it stopped. My doctor says these things happen sometimes. They don't mean anything."

I'm impressed by her apparent calm under pressure. "Next time let me know."

"What, you need more to worry about?"

"Listen, I'm already worrying about Em, what's a little more worry?"

She laughs and I realize we haven't chatted like this for years — since before Em was born.

When the phone rings, she snaps upright. I pick up the receiver, listen for a moment, then hold it out to her. "It's for you. Jim."

While she's on the phone I wander into the kitchen, the site of so much drama earlier today. There's still a pattern of spilled water on the floor, the carafe sits forlornly on the counter — the only clues to what happened here.

While I'm wiping up the floor, Mother appears to tell me, "It's all settled. I spoke with Jim and he's going to drop Emily off here at 5:30, and I'll bring her back at 8:00."

"Good, Mother. I'm glad you did that."

"Don't expect me to make a practice of this sort of thing," she says. "I'm not going soft in the head or sentimental or anything."

"I don't think you're going soft anywhere. And I want to thank you for your advice."

"My advice?"

"Remember you were telling me how to sell my author on the changes I want to make? He seems to be coming around to my way of thinking."

"I told you it would work out."

"Yes, you did."


When Jim arrives to pick up Em later that evening, I meet him at the door. "She's watching the end of a TV show," I tell him. "Five more minutes."

"Just what did you say to your mother to effect such a change?" he asks, leaning against the door frame.

"I told her I don't have the time to run back and forth between you two and if she wants to see Em, she has to talk to you. We're all grown-ups. It was getting ridiculous."

"She was actually not outright insulting to me," he says. "Although it would be pushing it to say she was warm and friendly."

"Maybe it's not true what they say about leopards and their

spots. Anyway, I want to talk to you about something."

"Oh?" He cocks an eyebrow. I can feel him withdraw, see his smile evaporate, hear the coolness in his voice.

"Nothing bad," I say. "I just think it's time you and I sorted some things out, tied up a few loose ends."

"You think so?" Suddenly he's very interested in a patch of grass at his feet.

"Yes, I do." I know it's not going to finish anything. As long as there's Em, he and I will be involved, but it's time to resolve some details and move on. It's partly my fault things dragged on this long. "I think I was sort of hoping we could work things out and get back together eventually, but that's not going to happen."

"No." He's still intent on the grass.

"And you're spinning your wheels because you're afraid once we're divorced you'll get married again and screw up a second time."

He looks up, amused. "You never were one to mince words."

"It's genetic," I say. "So once I get Spencer's book cleared up, we'll sit down and finalize things?"

Jim nods.

"How about over a dinner at Chez Nous, with a really good bottle of wine?"

He laughs. "Sounds good."

# Chapter 16

WHEN I GET TO THE OFFICE Tuesday morning, I discover that overnight Spencer has made changes that will require further fine-tuning of the manuscript. At this point, we're working line to line, word to word — a process similar to accentuating the salient details in a drawing by deepening shadows or picking out highlights. This time it is almost pleasant. The Spencer who sits across the table from me is quiet and focussed on the manuscript. There are no flashes of charm, no flirtatious remarks, no sexual undercurrent.

I pop out at one point to ask Jerri how the search for the missing package is going. She's on the phone. I stand around for a while, jot "Bristol?" on a piece of scrap paper and slide it in front of her. She nods, pointing to the phone. Covering the mouthpiece with her hand, she whispers, "I'm talking to the courier. They have me on hold."

"Catch you later," I say, retreating back into Hill's office.

Spencer and I work all morning. I take a coffee break at 10:30 to see if Jerri's got any further information about the missing package, but she's nowhere to be found. Janine has no idea where she is, so I leave a short note on her desk: "Bristol? Any news?" and return to Spencer.

At noon I order in lunch. Jerri is still missing, and the note I left sits untouched on her desk. Is she hiding from me? Has she run off? Has she been kidnapped by aliens? All are equally likely.

At 5:30 Spencer and I call it a day. Still no sign of Jerri. I head home where I spend the evening tying up loose ends and printing off a clean copy of *Sound and Silence* before climbing into bed at a reasonable hour for the first time in almost a week. In my dreams courier packages fly through the air and swoop out of reach when I try to grab them.

A light glaze of fog softens the world's contours when I glance out the kitchen window Wednesday morning. I have a quick bite, then it's time to get organized: purse, right here; briefcase, got it. How much cash do I have? Do I need to hit the bank machine on the way? No, I've got enough for lunch. Keys? Drat. Maybe in my jacket pocket? Bingo.

Out the door — just a moment. Where is the novel that's at the root of this crisis — the pages I printed out last night? It was on the kitchen table. No longer. By the phone? Damn, no. I dig through piles of paper. I'm about to give up entirely and redecorate the house in desperation when I focus on the jug of milk sitting beside my briefcase. A quick glance in the fridge; there sits the manuscript. I see. A little mix-up. The old neurons are crossed, are they? I stash the milk in the fridge, the manuscript in the briefcase, my coat on my back and the key in the front door lock. Click, and I'm off down the street.

I need a coffee. If I don't get more caffeine into my system quickly, I will grind to a halt in the middle of the sidewalk long before I make it to the office. The one cup I've already had is barely enough to get my engine turning over. Ah, help is in sight — straight ahead lies the Café Roma, haven of espresso, cappuccino, café latte and other necessities of life like fiorentino, flaky Napoleon pastries and buttery croissants.

I'm scant yards away from it when the door opens, releasing a customer. A cloud of coffee-scented air surrounds me, welcomes me, buoys me up as I enter.

"Coffee to go?" the woman behind the counter asks. I nod.

As I stand there, a voice says, "Elaine."

*Do I owe anyone money?* is my first thought. My second thought is, *that sounds like Nathan.*

I glance around but don't see anyone I recognize, just the regular crowd of grizzled old solidly built Mediterranean men with dark complexions and glittering black eyes who always occupy the same table at the back where they sit hunched over, muttering loudly and gesturing largely. I'm prepared to accept the fact that I've experienced an aural hallucination, when once again I hear, "Elaine?"

The woman on my right nudges me with her elbow and jerks her thumb sideways.

"Good morning."

"Nathan!" I'm surprised at the rush of warmth I feel, how genuinely happy I am to see him. My voice sounds foolishly loud to me.

"Hello." Do I delude myself, or does he sound pleased, too?

"Fancy meeting you here." *Ouch, Elaine. Can't you do better than that? Not on a Wednesday morning.* I pay for my coffee and wait while Nathan selects a Danish.

We step outside into tepid sunlight. "How's the book coming?" he asks.

"I guess it could be worse."

"I know what you mean," he says. "Before my divorce came through, I used to lie in bed at night and imagine how much easier life was going to be when the divorce was final. Then the day after we signed the papers, Jennifer, my ex-wife, wanted to change the access arrangements and everything blew up again. And I thought, *This isn't better. This is worse. I guess it could be even worse, but I don't know how.* That's when I realized that as long as we had this child together, my wife and I were going to be connected somehow."

I stand transfixed, listening to the real Nathan, catching a glimpse for an instant behind the facade he presents to the world. Questions elbow their way forward, demanding to be asked — *How long were you married? What was she like? What went wrong?* — but I stifle the impulse to quiz him, afraid I might scare him off before I have a chance to get to know him.

"For about ten minutes I considered joining the army," he says.

"Really?" The word blurts out before I can stop it. The idea of Nathan — at this moment wearing slouchy black corduroy pants, a deep green wool sweater and a battered leather jacket, hair raggle-taggle at shirt collar length — in uniform is so incongruous.

"Until I realized I couldn't stand being away from Isaac." He is reflective for a moment, and I wait.

*More,* I think. *I want to hear more about what you think and what you feel, more about the real Nathan.*

But when he looks up, his expression has shifted. "What will you do now? With Spencer's book, I mean?" he says.

I feel a twinge of disappointment — he's slipped away again. Once more his tone is reserved and distant; he's retreated into civility and commonplace.

I hope my regret isn't as apparent as I suspect it must be. "I think it could be publishable. Not great, but publishable."

He nods, seems to be about to say something, thinks better of it, smiles awkwardly, turns and walks away. I am left standing on the sidewalk alone staring after him with the distinct impression I've missed a cue somewhere along the line. Did I neglect to say something I should have? Did I say something I shouldn't have? It's all so confusing.

Oh well, my coffee's getting cold and time's a-wasting. Off to the office, into the breach. Onward, ever onward.

Soon the familiar facade is rising before me, the pockmarked front walk, the spindly Chinese elm hedge. I unlock the front door and let myself into the office, setting the manuscript on my desk. At 8:30 Spencer knocks on the office door. No sign of Jerri yet, but it's still early.

"Come on in." I usher him into Hill's office, and we settle down to work.

Mid-afternoon I walk down the hall and knock on the conference-room door.

"We're finished," I tell Hill. Down to the wire, but on time.

I follow in his wake as he barrels down the hall and practically lunges at the pile of paper sitting on the table in front of Spencer.

"Hi, Spencer," Hill says gruffly.

Spencer nods.

"Things satisfactory?"

Spencer glances from Hill to me. "Just fine," I say emphatically.

"Fine," echoes Spencer. "Ms. Salter's done a tremendous job on this."

Hill's gaze fixes on me as if I'm registering for the first time. Reading through the first few pages with lightning speed, he nods vigorously as he makes his way through the manuscript.

"This is good," he says to Spencer. "This is some of the best writing you've done."

"I, uh," Spencer stammers. But colour is flowing into his face; he is sitting up straighter.

"Trust me," Hill continues, picking up the rest of the manuscript possessively. Then he turns to me. "I can take it from here, Elaine. I've left the folder for the next project on your desk. I'll discuss it with you this afternoon." He turns away from me. I am dismissed.

Over Hill's shoulder I cast Spencer a glance. His eyes meet mine, then slide away. He's listening to Hill and nodding enthusiastically. As I step into the hall and pull the door quietly shut, Hill's voice floats after me. I hear the tag-end of a sentence, "— a print run of maybe 10,000." Then words that strike fear into my heart, "— and your *next* book —"

*Not another book,* I groan to myself walking down the hall. I pass Jerri, who has her ear to the phone, and dawdle by her desk until she's finished her conversation.

"Thanks for your help with the Spencer situation on Monday, Jerri — stashing him in Hill's office," I tell her. "It saved the day."

"No prob." She grins widely.

"Now, let's find out where this goddamned package is."

"Oh, I meant to tell you before I left yesterday for my craniosacral therapy session; the courier called. The package was never in Edmonton. It was delivered to Bristol two days ago, but I guess I forgot to put Ghislaine's name on the outside, so it sat at the front desk for a day, then it went to the wrong department. She's got it now and everything's cool."

"Craniosacral therapy," I say. "What's that like?"

"It's great. It completely empties my head — all the stresses and negativity just evaporate. That's why I was late today — I got so relaxed, I slept right through my alarm this morning. You should try it."

*No thank you,* I think. *One empty head in this office is enough.*

"Well, that's one fire put out," I tell her. "I'm sure another one's starting somewhere as we speak." Something occurs to me. "Did Janine get you the mailing list you asked for?"

"Yeah," Jerri says.

"Well, why don't you take care of the poetry launch? You could handle it on your own."

"God, no — I need a break. Mailing lists, couriers, printers, Hill. I have been so stressed."

*Stress is just life's way of telling you you're not dead yet,* I'm on the point of telling her. Instead, I smile and walk away. I guess my job is safe for a while longer.

By the time I reach my desk, I've decided that if Hill saddles me with Spencer's next book, the author will have to meet some conditions. I won't have any compunction about playing hardball if he starts acting up. This may be the beginning of a beautiful relationship — a beautiful *working* relationship.

What's next? Hill's left the folder for the next project on my desk, but there are a few loose ends that need tying up. First I have to nail down the details of excerpting *Sound and Silence* for *City.* Then I'm going to have to figure out how to present this to Hill. I don't want him to assume I'm going to pitch ideas to Paige all the time.

And after that? After that, I'm done revising romance. The i's are all dotted, the t's are all crossed, though no doubt there's a run-on sentence somewhere I've missed. Or an incomplete one. But it's out of my hands now; Hill will do the final edit, mark the changes and corrections he wants made. Typeset, proofed and off to the printers.

And it's back to the gritty black-and-white realities of quotidian life. So much for excitement, so much for drama. No more late-night sessions. Buckle down to the usual round: bed at a reasonable hour, getting up with the sun, going to work. Em will be back home tonight, which means there will be laundry to be washed, meals to be cooked, homework to nag about. Once again romance has travelled a fleeting trajectory through my life: the romance and excitement of publishing, of working to an excruciatingly tight deadline, of trying to turn a sow's ear into a silk purse. The romance of will-the-author-won't-the-author co-operate, will-I-won't-I lose my job.

Then there's the other type of romance. I like Nathan, but you can't call what has passed between us romance.

Which is just as well. I've had enough of that kind of romance anyway. I'm not looking for sparks like the ones that flew between Jim and me at the beginning. I don't need the disruption that falling in love entails, don't need the static. I'm happy just to get on quietly with life, head down, nose to the grindstone. Being employed is good — in this economic climate, I'm lucky to have a job. Hormones abating will be good — I look forward to the end of the monthly roller-coaster ride. Over the past twenty years, I've probably wasted thousands of dollars on impulse purchases in the week before my period. Exactly how many pairs of shoes does one woman need, anyway? Once menopause sets in, maybe I'll be able to save some money. I'll stop plucking my eyebrows, stop shaving my legs. I'll put my energy into good works, or sublimate it watching my daughter grow up gracefully.

Except ... maybe I'm not quite ready to kiss romance goodbye. Maybe it would be nice to have a little more fun before the Big Editor in the sky decides my story has run its course. I could enjoy a little sizzle. At a lower wattage than I was looking for in my twenties, but a flash of something — and I'm not thinking of something of the hot menopausal kind, either.

Something soft and gentle is what I'm looking for, like the shifting glow of the northern lights — that slightly mysterious non-light which by its presence makes the darkness around it habitable and enticing; makes night a garment to wrap around yourself, not a waning of the light.

# Chapter 17

WHILE HILL REMAINS closeted with Spencer, I send Paige an e-mail outlining the results of our strategy. Then I settle down to work on my next project, the biography of a well known singer-songwriter, a *poet maudit* whose voice sounds like my car's engine struggling to life on a cold winter morning, metal grinding on frozen metal. The troubadour of disillusion and love gone wrong, he does have a certain *je ne sais quoi,* although I'm not sure I want to *sais,* since prolonged exposure to his music makes me think seriously about slitting my wrists.

After Jim moved out, I listened to his songs for hours. I'd lie supine beside the stereo on the living-room floor, committing to memory the pattern of cracks and puckers on the ceiling above me. Whenever a tape finished, I'd pop in another one and stare at the ceiling some more, sinking back into despair. I hadn't realized how thoroughly this music had saturated my life until Em and I were driving somewhere recently. I snapped a tape of his music into the car stereo, and Em knew every word of every song by heart. It makes me wonder what else has filtered into that brain of hers when I'm not looking.

After half an hour, I hear Hill's firm tread coming down the hall. He stops by my desk and says, "It's looking good, but Spencer's made a few more changes and I've got to get it marked up. A couple more days and this should be all tied up." As he disappears into his office, he barks over his shoulder, "Tomorrow at 9:15." Then his office door shuts firmly behind him.

*Fine by me,* I think, and turn my attention back to the world of shattered promises and tattered curtains. Is it my imagination, or do the books I've been working on recently share a theme: love, the fallout attendant upon it, and its inevitable failure?

At 5:00 I tuck the poet away for the night, tidy my desk, turn my desk calendar to tomorrow's date and pencil "Meet w/Hill" in the 9:00 a.m. slot. Slinging on my coat and slipping my purse over my shoulder, I call, "See you in the morning," to Jerri and step out into the end of a shimmering autumn day.

The late afternoon sun bathes storefronts in a warm amber-tinted light. Glass glistens, metal surfaces shine, peoples' faces take on a glow of well-being. The warmth, the glorious golden radiance of the sun makes me feel slightly drifty and purposeless, but I have an apology to make, so I start off toward Palimpsest.

Pictures begin to drift through my mind: Nathan coming into focus through the gloom of the store; Nathan offering me a pan of lasagne; Nathan standing behind Isaac, his hand resting protectively on his son's shoulder; Nathan at the door Saturday evening. Yes, even *I* can recognize the common denominator here.

I'm not exactly sure what's going on, but I know I feel comfortable with him. Nathan tried to warn me about Spencer and I kept cutting him off. I kept pushing him away. At the very least, I want to tell him what's happened and see where it goes from there. I know where I'd like it to go, but I realize I could be setting myself up for disappointment.

As I age, I notice myself acquiring an increasing number of idiosyncrasies — wearing socks to bed, folding towels just so — that stick to me like barnacles. It's probably the same with Nathan. What hope is there that two barnacle-encrusted individuals can get close enough to hug, let alone find comfort in each other's arms?

And yet, I figure as long as there's room for change, there's room for hope. Take Mother, for example. She never ceases to surprise me. The peace deal she brokered with Jim — will wonders never cease? And watching her with Em is a revelation. I try to understand how they've managed to achieve the easy bantering relationship they share. If Mother criticizes Em's table manners or corrects her pronunciation, Em laughs it off or engulfs her in a hug that smothers Mother's words.

Em's self-assurance and Mother's response to it suggest the possibility of change. I doubt Mother and I will ever be on the phone to each other every day, but who knows — I'm picking up a few pointers from Em. If my recent behaviour is any indication, maybe there are other things you can inherit from your children besides grey hair. If there's hope in this, there may be hope in other areas, too.

I reach the block where Palimpsest is located and stop in front of the bead shop next door so I can watch Nathan without being observed. In the starting-to-fade daylight, I peer through the window. He sits with his back to the street, intent on a book of some sort. He reads slowly, flipping the pages back and forth thoughtfully. There's something reassuring in how deliberate his movements are, how considered.

I know what comes next, and a riff of excitement runs up my back. But at the same time, another emotion plays in counterpoint behind the exhilaration. Not as heavy as sadness, exactly, but *tristesse,* a shadow of melancholy about Jim and me, and how we came to grief.

I remember how strong I felt, heady with the rush of confidence new love confers, when Jim and I were first involved. The world could toss anything my way, and I knew I could field it. The end was sad, wresting back a part of myself I hadn't realized I'd given away. Now my next step will take me into new territory, and I feel like I'm saying goodbye to my life with Jim, or at least closing it off in some way. There is a sense of lightening, a weight lifting from my shoulders, but also of something passing. But now it's time to step forward, take a risk and start something new.

In the window of the bead store I catch my reflection, stoop-shouldered. *Stand up straight,* I tell myself, trying to ignore the knot of nervousness in my stomach, *what have you got to lose?* I push open the door of Palimpsest purposefully.

Interrupted, Nathan glances up briefly, then returns to his reading. After a moment he looks up again. "Elaine," he says. "To what do I owe the honour of this visit?"

"Do you always talk like a book?" *Jeez, Elaine. Does everything that pops into your head have to pop out of your mouth?*

"Only when I'm feeling self-conscious," he replies evenly.

"Fair enough." Silence for a moment. "I just dropped by to apologize."

He frowns. "For what?"

"For cutting you off Sunday night when you tried to talk to me about Spencer. For cutting you off generally."

"No, no." Nathan shakes his head. "You shouldn't. It was ridiculous of me —" He breaks off.

I cough.

Nathan looks at me questioningly.

"All that stuff I said about being able to look after myself — he got under my radar." I shrug somewhat sheepishly. "You were right — Spencer's a worm. After I made that tremendously empowered speech, he put the moves on me on Monday."

Nathan puts the book down on the counter and leans forward. "What happened?"

I tell him the whole story: Spencer's behaviour, my response, the resolution.

When I finish, he observes, "Spencer can be charming when he wants to, so it's not hard to see why he might fool you."

"Well, I'm sorry I've been cutting you short."

"There was something I started to tell you the other night, but I couldn't." He pauses for a moment, then continues. "Jennifer and I came here so she could go to university. The English department has a good reputation. We got to know Spencer and Catherine well. He was new to the department. They hadn't been married very long; neither had we. The four of us got along well, and we ended up spending a lot of time together.

"Then Isaac was born." His voice deepens with warmth, a smile spreads across his face. "But after that, things got tough. Jennifer was at school, the bookstore was going through a rough patch. We juggled child care. It seemed like there was never enough money or enough time or enough sleep." He stops. "But I'm boring you."

He's about to disappear into politeness again, so I lean forward and rest my hand on his arm. "No, you're not."

"When Isaac was two, Jennifer told me she and Spencer had been having an affair. For about a year. She told me she'd called it off and she wanted us to patch things up and make a new start. So we tried — at least, I did. Six months later I found out she was still sleeping with Spencer. I told her to leave. It was the most difficult time of my life." Nathan stops. His face is hard. "Once she was on her own, Spencer got cold feet and refused to see her. Ten months later — a year — she met a woman and they moved in together. They planned to do a lot of travelling, so she didn't contest it when I went for sole custody.

"I thought about moving out of town after Jennifer and I split, but I'd made a life here, and this is Isaac's home. I didn't want to leave. And then I met you at one of the Hunter Press book launches." He grins. "When you came into the store the other day and I found out you were working with Spencer, I wanted to tell you everything, but I couldn't — I've gotten so used to not talking about it."

"Thanks for your concern. What I don't understand in this whole thing is Catherine, his wife. Why does she stay?"

"She loves him," Nathan replies simply. "Catherine loves Spencer."

"It's that simple?"

He gives me a measuring look. "I don't think it's simple. I don't think love's simple, do you?"

I think of Jim, of Em, of my mother, of all the different shadings and inflections of love I've felt for each of them; love flooded with passion or tinged with rage or coloured by frustration. I think about how the laws of Heisenberg's theories seem to have some relevance to relationships: no one on the outside of one knows what's really going on inside it. The moment you start observing a relationship, you change the dynamics of it. Sometimes how it works and what holds it together are mysteries even to the participants. At the heart of every relationship is a mystery.

"No," I shake my head. "No, it's not simple. Love isn't simple at all."

He comes around from behind the counter and stands in front of me. "There's something else I think I should warn you about," he says.

"What?"

He pulls me close and puts his arms around me. He smells of leather and woodsmoke. Then his mouth is on mine, and the kiss is long and slow and just right. There is hunger and comfort and pleasure in it, and when we finish, I take a long, contented breath.

"That." He grins.

"Why don't you warn me one more time?" I smile.

Afterwards he reaches over and flips the "Open" sign in the window to "Closed."

"I'll walk you home if you want," he says, shutting the cash register and pulling his jacket off the back of his stool. Ushering me before him out of the shop, he pulls the door shut behind us and locks it.

"You're closing?" I say. "Won't you lose business?"

Nathan smiles wryly and shakes his head. "*My* busy time is *after* Christmas. All those wrong guesses, you know."

For a second we stand face-to-face in the doorway without speaking. "Shall we go?" he suggests.

We set out at a relaxed pace, heading west on Princess Street. "So the book is in the bag?" he asks.

"Yes," I say, realizing it's true. "I can't quite believe it, but it is. Spencer took the changes, most of them — the big ones."

"Good." He walks beside me, hands jammed deep into his jacket pockets. We turn north on Clergy Street.

"So, Nathan," I say, dizzy with the recklessness of it. "If I were to go looking for gossip, what would be out there on you?"

He considers the question for the time it takes us to walk the block from Princess Street to Queen Street. I almost think I've lost him when he replies, "I suppose it would depend on who you asked."

At the corner we wait for a break in traffic. "Isaac told me this morning I'm a pretty good dad, but I'd be a great one if I got him a certain computer game he's had his eye on." A space opens in the flow of cars and we dart across the street. When we reach the other side, he continues. "Jennifer said I didn't travel enough. We didn't take enough vacations."

"She thought you were a workaholic?"

Nathan snorts. "No one can accuse me of that. No, she just told me one day we didn't take enough vacations. Then she got bored with that. Now she's studying massage therapy and natural healing." He sighs wistfully. "Sometimes it's depressing to think you were just a phase in someone else's life."

He's silent as we walk along, then adds, "Marriage isn't easy all the time — ours wasn't — but I was always in it for the long haul. I don't think you get over someone you've loved," he says. "I think you just incorporate them into your life, grow around them the way a tree grows around a wound."

At the park we stop. For a moment we stand side by side, pointedly not looking at each other. There are so many things I want to say, I'm struck dumb. After a minute of silence, I'm about to blurt, *well, so long,* give him what I hope is a noncommittal smile, turn right, toward home — but at that instant, he puts his hand on my arm and says, "Come home with me, Elaine." There is an intensity to his voice that surprises me. "For a cup of coffee," he adds quickly. "It's not far — just a couple of blocks that way," he says, nodding northward. "Isaac will be there, and the baby-sitter," he adds.

I take a deep breath. "Sure," I reply as I exhale, the word rising like hope. I fall into step beside him. We walk through the park and down the hill on the other side in silence. At the bottom of the hill, we turn onto a tree-lined street. The houses here are unpretentious but tidy. Nathan stops in front of a modest two-storey white wood frame house with a maple tree in the front yard and a convoy of toy cars and trucks littering the driveway.

We stand on the sidewalk in front of the house for what seems like a long time but is probably only a few seconds.

"Come on in," Nathan says. He's not smiling, but I read amusement in his eyes. "Nothing out of the ordinary in there, just one babysitter who will be very grateful I'm home early, and a Lego-obsessed eleven-year-old." He holds out his hand to me.

I reach for it. The air between us quickens. Our fingers touch. I feel something jump between us — a spark or jolt. Of what — energy? Free-floating angst? I glance at Nathan to gauge his reaction, but his face is hidden from me, turned toward the house.

Maybe it's my imagination, I tell myself, or maybe, considering the time of the year, it's static electricity.

Or maybe not. Nathan stops, turns back. He's smiling now. A

tightness I was unaware of loosens its grip on me and falls away. I smile at him, then I'm laughing, feeling light-headed as we walk inside. *This is possible,* I think. *This just might fly.*

∞